1.

On THE LIP of the grim gorge of Pecos Canyon, Jim Hatfield, whom a Lieutenant in the Texas Rangers had dubbed the Lone Wolf, sat upon his golden sorrel. Far below him, the Pecos River foamed and thundered its way to the Rio Grande. Behind him was a steep slope to the rimrock. A mile downstream, the old iron bridge that spanned the river rose between its rock walls.

The slope flowing up to the rimrock and the far lip of the canyon were dotted with bristles of thicket and occasional trees. In the shadow of the slope to the western rimrock ran a trail.

The sky was flaming with the scarlet and gold of the sunset which played strange and glorious fires on the crest of the rimrock. The depths of the gorge were filling with purple shadows that climbed higher and higher. Through their misty curtain could be seen flashes of white as the river stormed the rocks.

"Quite a country, Goldy," Hatfield remarked to the sorrel. "She hasn't changed much in fifty years. Just about the same as what my grandfather used to tell about. And I reckon the people haven't changed much, either. Still some good, still some bad. And the good and the bad are still fighting it out to judge from the reports coming into headquarters of late. Well, Captain McDowell 'lowed we'd likely have an interesting time over here before we got things straightened out.

Looks peaceful enough right now, though. But I've a
notion it'll be sort of different a few miles to the west.
Bowman, I believe it's called."

Hatfield made a striking picture as he sat his great
horse in the red blaze of the sunet. Very tall—well over
six feet—his broad shoulders and strong chest tapered
to a lean, sinewy waist and hips. About his waist were
double cartridge belts. From the carefully oiled and
worked, cut-out holsters suspended from the belts the
plain black butts of heavy guns protruded. His costume
was the homely but efficient garb of the rangeland—
faded overalls and shirt, batwing chaps, well scuffed
half-boots of softly tanned leather, broad-brimmed
"J.B.," vivid neckerchief looped about his sinewy
throat. His coat was strapped with his blanket roll behind the cantle of his saddle.

The Lone Wolf's face was as arresting as his form
and was dominated by long, level eyes of a peculiar
shade of green that peered from beneath heavy black
brows. His hair, revealed by his pushed-back hat, was
also black with a crisp look to it. His nose was promi-
nent, his chin and jaw long and powerful. His rather
wide mouth, turned up at the corners, somewhat relieved the grimness of the hawk nose and the lean jaw.

Hooking one leg over the saddle horn, Hatfield
lounged comfortably and rolled a cigarette. Smoking
thoughtfully, he gazed northward along the winding
stretch of trail. Suddenly his eyes grew interested. A
single horseman had rounded a bend about a mile distant and was speeding south.

"That jigger sure is sifting sand," Hatfield muttered.
"Looks like he must be late for supper."

Still mildly interested, the Lone Wolf watched the
approach of the distant horseman. Then abruptly his
interest grew intense. He straightened in the hull and
stared northward.

Around the bend had bulged five more horsemen
also going like the wind. And even as Hatfield gazed,

whitish puffs of smoke mushroomed from their close ranks.

Rigid with excitement, Hatfield watched the grisly drama unfold. The fugitive, bending low in his saddle, urged his tall black horse to frantic speed. Behind him, gaining slowly, thundered the pursuit, rifles flaming.

"What in blazes?" muttered the Ranger. "Sheriff's posse chasing an owlhoot? Looks that way. Too much so for me to take a chance on interfering, even if I could. Chances are they'll down him before he gets opposite me and till he does, the range is too far for me to do anything about it."

Tensely he estimated the width of the gorge as the man in front closed the distance. He was almost opposite Hatfield when the end came. Suddenly, as the rifles blazed and crackled, he spun from his saddle, struck the lip of the gorge and rolled over. The Ranger's breath caught in his throat as the limp form plummeted downward. Then he exclaimed aloud as he saw what was hidden from the exultantly whooping pursuers.

The wounded man's body crashed through a bristle of growth jutting out from the gorge wall, shunted inward and came to rest on a narrow ledge perhaps a score of feet below the lip, there to lie supine and motionless save for a slight fluttering of his hands.

Hatfield raised his eyes from the limp form huddled beneath the concealing growth. The pursuing horsemen were almost opposite him now. He could make out the white blotches of faces turned in his direction. The reflected sunlight glinted on shifted metal. At the same instant the Ranger went sideways from his saddle. His hand gripped the stock of the heavy Winchester snugged in the saddle boot beneath his left thigh. The long gun was in his grasp when he hit the ground a split second later.

"Cover, Goldy!" he shouted as lead yelled through the air.

The sorrel streaked for the nearby growth.

Huddled against a little ridge of earth at the very lip of the gorge, Hatfield threw the rifle to his shoulder. His eyes, coldly gray, glinted along the sights. Bullets were kicking up spurts of dust within yards of where he lay. Others whined past so close he felt their lethal breath. Then the big Winchester boomed suddenly.

Across the gorge a man reeled in his saddle, clutching the horn for support. Taking careful aim, Hatfield fired a second time. He did not hear the yelp of pain the shot brought, but he saw another horseman grab at his shoulder. He shifted the rifle muzzle the merest trifle and squeezed the stock.

But now the troop was under way, bending low in their saddles, quirting their horses. Smoke spurted from the rifle muzzle. A hat sailed through the air and went tossing and tumbling into the depths of the gorge, a grayish blur against the dark background of the rock.

Hatfield tore out the spent shells, staring at the re- treating riders, noting every peculiarity of form and horsemanship. He observed that the first man, appar- ently the leader, was tall, lean, broad-shouldered, a superb rider, who sat his mount as if he were a part of the animal. In the rear rode a hulking individual with bowed shoulders and out-thrust neck. He heaved his shoulders with each spring of the horse, as if he were lifting the animal along rather than being carried by it.

"Couldn't get a look at their faces—too far—but little things sometimes crop up and turn out to be big things," Hatfield muttered as he tipped the rifle muzzle up and sent three more slugs whining after the discom- fited riders who were flogging their horses down the trail at top speed. "Well, looked like I winged a couple of 'em and threw a helluva scare into the one that lost his hat. Reckon that's enough for the time being. Now what's this all about? No sheriff's posse, that's for cer- tain! Appears they didn't like the looks of a witness over on this side. If I hadn't been keeping a close watch on the hellions, that first slug would likely have punctured my hide. It went right over Goldy's back." ‾

He stood up, his attention centered on the man who lay below the canyon lip.

"Wonder if the poor devil is done for?" he mused. "Doesn't appear to be moving any more, not even his hands. That's for the best, though, if he's alive. If he starts flopping around he's got a good chance of going over the edge and landing in the river, and that's a mighty long drop. Reckon I'd better try and make it across."

2.

THE GUN-SLINGERS had vanished from sight around a bend a quarter of a mile or so downstream. Hatfield gazed toward the spot where he had last seen the galloping horses. Satisfied that they had disappeared, he whistled a shrill note. Goldy came trotting from behind the thicket where he had sought cover at his master's command. Hatfield forked him and sent him downstream at a moderate pace.

"The question is," he thought, "did those jiggers turn west over the rimrock or will they cross the bridge to this side? Don't want to barge into them unexpectedly. Five to one is sort of long odds even if a couple of them don't happen to be feeling so good about now. Even if he's near dead, that kind is still as dangerous as a broken-back rattler."

Farther along there was considerable growth back of the gorge lip. Hatfield took advantage of the cover it offered and approached the bridge warily. When he sighted it about ten minutes later the rickety-looking span was deserted. And the far approach was free of dry growth that might have afforded the gunmen concealment.

"Good enough," the Ranger muttered. "Looks like they turned west and went over the rim."

A little later Goldy's irons were clattering on the floor boards. They reached the far shore without encountering anyone. With a glance at the rimrock glowing redly against the sunset sky, Hatfield turned the sorrel's nose upstream and sent him along at a fast clip. He easily spotted the place where the wounded man had gone over the edge. Then he noted something else—dark smudges marked the gray dust of the trail.

"Buzzard I winged appears to be losing considerable blood," he decided. "Not bright arterial blood, though. Flow likely to stop by itself. But just the same I've a notion he feels the need of a doctor. Which might give me a chance to get a line on him in town, if they stop there. Hold it, Goldy, here's where that fellow went over."

Pulling the sorrel to a halt, he dismounted and peered over the lip. He could see now that the drop was not quite sheer but sloped back a trifle toward the edge of the cliff. Moreover, just above the clump of growth was a slight bulge that hid the ledge on which the wounded man had rested when Hatfield last saw him.

The Lone Wolf glanced about, his black brows drawing together. There was no tree or protruding rock to which he might hitch his rope; for it was plain that to reach the man on the ledge he must go down the twine hand over hand. The slope was too steep for him to clamber down.

"Well, Goldy, I guess it's up to you," he told the sorrel. "And don't slip or somebody else will be riding you from now on."

Unlooping the sixty-foot twine, he tied it hard and fast to the saddle horn. Then he dangled the slender rope down through the growth.

"Here we go," he said, and eased over the lip.

Goldy snorted in protest as the Ranger's two hundred pounds of bone and muscle creaked the horn and strained the cinches.

"You haven't seen anything yet," Hatfield told him grimly. "Steady, feller!"

Sliding, slipping and bumping against the rock face of the cliff, he slid gently downward. A moment more and he was thrashing and worming his way through the hindering growth. In the deepening shadow he could just make out the sprawled and motionless form of the man lying on the narrow ledge. He worked down a little farther and managed to find a precarious balance on the rough stone. Clinging to the rope with one hand, he bent over the wounded man.

"Still breathing, anyhow," he muttered. " 'Pears to be badly hit, though, the way he's gasping."

He leaned closer and uttered a low exclamation. The heavy slug had struck the man in the head slightly below the hairline and a little back of the left temple. His face was a mask of drying blood. The grizzled hair on the top of his head was matted with it. The bullet had gone clean through at a sharp angle, emerging near the crown.

"Should have killed him, but it didn't," Hatfield growled. "May have a chance if I can get him to a doctor in time. But that's not going to be easy. Thank Pete he isn't very big. Maybe I can do it."

Swiftly he considered a plan of procedure. He did not dare loop the rope under the man's shoulders and haul him up the slope. That would be easy enough; but the risk of striking the wounded head against the bulge above or against one of the tangled branches of the growth was too great. Any additional injury would

surely prove fatal, Hatfield believed. There was just
one thing to do.

Teetering on the narrow ledge, he gently straightened the man's arms above his head. Then he slipped
the loop of his rope over the wrists and drew the noose
tight. Next, by a miracle of balance and agility and the
expenditure of every ounce of his great strength, he
got the bound arms around his own neck and straightened up with the limp form dangling down his back.
The pressure of the noosed wrists against his throat
was throttling but he finally worked them down far
enough to allow him to breathe. Then he gripped the
dangling rope with both hands and started the terrible
climb up the jagged wall.

"Steady, boy, steady!" he called hoarsely as he heard
Goldy's irons slip and scrape on the stone above.

A frightened snort answered him, but the big horse
kept his footing. The great weight kept him slipping
and sliding, however, which was not at all reassuring
to Hatfield as he strained one hand over the other and
inched slowly up the cliff. The shadows were thick now
and the deepening gloom did not make the going any
easier. Getting through the growth and over the bulge
was a terrific struggle. Sweat streamed down Hatfield's
face. His body was wet with it and his shirt clung clam-
mily to his back and shoulders as the bulging muscles
threatened to split the seams. The twenty feet he had
negotiated so swiftly and easily when sliding down to
the edge abruptly stretched out into whole furlongs
and time seemed to stand still in a black void of
pain and agonizing effort. Gasping for breath as the
throttling wrists pressed against his windpipe, he
struggled upward in spasmodic jerks. Once his hand,
wet with sweat, slipped on the thin rope and for a terrible instant he thought he had lost his hold. The black
depths and the roaring white water yawned beneath.
Above, the first stars were glinting golden in the blue-
purple sky. The lip of the gorge was a dark line that

seemed to waver and recede before his straining eyes.

And then, with a final agony of effort, he was over the edge, flat on his face in the dust of the trail with the leaden weight of the rescued man on top of him.

But now the strangling pressure was removed from his throat. He gulped in great draughts of life-giving air and his strength quickly returned. He managed to release the man's wrists and carefully wriggled from under him.

"Still breathing, anyhow," he muttered. "An old fellow, but he looks strong and wiry. I've a notion he's got a chance if I can get him to a doctor in a hurry."

He carefully examined the wound and shook his head. The bleeding had stopped, he noted with satisfaction. But although he had a certain knowledge of medicine, such an injury was beyond his skill. He contented himself with binding a handkerchief around the wounded head and washing the blood from the man's face with a little water from his canteen.

There was no sign of the man's horse. Hatfield recalled that it had streaked off down the trail when its master fell. Doubtless it had headed for its home range, wherever that was. At any rate it would have been of no use under the circumstances. The man was too badly injured to risk roping him to the hull. Hatfield decided the only safe method was to cradle him in his arms. With considerable difficulty he managed to mount the sorrel, holding the limp form against his breast. Then he sent Goldy down the trail at a smooth running walk. When he reached the bridge he turned west, following a well-defined track that climbed the long slope to the rimrock. It was completely dark now and the sky was a glory of stars that glowed like grapes of golden light in the vast blue-black bowl of the heavens. As yet there was no moon. However, it didn't matter, for the trail was good and ran almost straight.

Hatfield's face was grim as he rode, for he was thinking of just such another ride he had taken, quite a few years before, with a limp form cradled against his breast, the body of his own father. But that time he was not speeding for a doctor's help. The elder Hatfield was dead, callously slain by wideloopers who had run off his herd. And young Jim Hatfield, just out of engineering college, had vowed revenge. But before he could start to ride the vengeance trail, Captain Bill McDowell had sent for him. Hatfield seemed to hear the old Ranger Captain's quiet voice seeping through the steady drum of Goldy's hoofs as he pointed out the dangers of the course Hatfield had set for himself.

"Just one little slip and you're on the wrong side of the law," Captain Bill had said. "Taking the law into your own hands is a mighty risky business, no matter how justified you may think you are. All of a sudden you're an owlhoot just like the ones you're chasing, and once you're riding *that* trail, it's almighty hard to turn back. Your father was my friend, Jim, and I want to save you from that. Tell you what—come into the Rangers. Then you'll have the law and all the power and prestige of the State of Texas back of you. The very first chore I'll give you will be that of running down your dad's killers. A chance to do it in the right way."

Hatfield's lips twitched a little as he recalled the crafty old Captain's next words—

"Of course, after you finish the chore, you'll be free to leave the outfit and go ahead and be an engineer like you've planned, if you're a mind to."

That was what Captain Bill said. But running down his father's killers and bringing them to justice had been a long chore, and by the time it was finished, Jim Hatfield was a Ranger. And he had never regretted it. He still planned to be a civil engineer some day, and had kept up his studies with that end in view. But as yet he was not ready to leave the Rangers. The Lone Wolf had become legend throughout the Southwest, honored, admired and respected by honest men, hated and feared by the outlaw brand. There always seemed to be a new chore ready for Captain Bill's Lieutenant and ace-man. Always some place where decent people were in need of help, where evil must be stamped out. The war was never-ending, and how can a good soldier quit when there's a war going on?

3.

As soon as Hatfield reached the rimrock he saw, perhaps two miles ahead, a cluster of lights that undoubtedly marked the site of the cowtown of Bowman. Down the winding trail of the far sag he sent Goldy. Less than half an hour later he was on the outskirts of the town.

It was a typical cow country town—a rather broad main street lined with adobes and ramshackle frame buildings, most of them false fronts. Lanterns hung on poles provided makeshift street lighting that was reinforced by bars of radiance streaming through windows and over the tops of swinging doors. Every other building, it seemed, housed a saloon, gambling den, or dance-hall, with an occasional restaurant or general store to relieve the monotony.

Pulling up, Hatfield stopped a passer-by and asked for the location of a doctor's office.

"Right straight ahead," said the man, staring at the limp burden in Hatfield's arms. "You can't miss it—right-hand side of the street. There's a sign on the window. Doc Beard is the name. What happened?"

"Fellow got hurt," Hatfield replied tersely. The man

peered at the wounded man's face and started back with an exclamation. As Hatfield rode on, he stood staring and muttering. Then he turned and fairly ran down a side street.

After passing three intersections, Hatfield sighted the doctor's office in a squat little building. A light glowed through the window. He dismounted carefully, left Goldy securely tethered to the evening breeze and mounted the two steps to the door. He kicked the panel hard and waited.

There was a clumping of boots inside, a rumbling growl and the door swung open revealing a white-whiskered old fellow with a pair of truculent blue eyes set deep beneath shaggy brows. He held a lamp high and peered searchingly at the tall Ranger and his grisly burden.

"What the hell?" he bellowed.

"Fellow got shot," Hatfield cut in, and stepped through the door.

"Another one!" snorted the old doctor, placing the lamp on a nearby table and glaring at Hatfield as if he were personally responsible for everything that had been going wrong.

"Another one!" he repeated. "What the hell's goin' on around here. Just worked over two, not half an hour ago. One had a bad hole through his shoulder and the other one had lost about half a rib and a pound or two of meat. Both in bad shape. Ought to be in bed. Insisted on riding off soon as I tied 'em up."

Rumbling through his whiskers he bent forward and peered at the wounded man's face. He recoiled a step, his eyes wide.

"Good God!" he gasped, "It's Bill Carter! What—how—"

"Never mind that," Hatfield replied. "We'll talk later. This man is badly hurt and needs attention. He's shot through the head."

Instantly the doctor sobered.

"Bring him into the next room," he ordered. "Lay him down on that couch. Careful now, don't jar him. Let me have a look. Hold that lamp, will you?"

He bent over the ashen face, examined the wound with deft fingers and swore some more.

"Bad, damn bad," he said. "Wonder he's still alive, but he is." He lifted a limp wrist and felt for the pulse, then laid his ear against the man's laboring chest. He straightened up, still growling curses, and jerked open a drawer.

"Heart stimulant right away," he said. "See if that water on the stove is boiling. Should be. I was just getting ready to clean up after patching those two cowhands. Okay?"

He drew forth a hypodermic needle and a small vial. "Damn this hand of mine!" he growled. "I can hardly use it. Horse stepped on it while I was rubbing him down. Handling nitroglycerin with busted fingers is a tough chore." He fumbled the stopper of the vial free with his teeth.

"Just a minute," Hatfield said. "I figure I can administer that injection. My hands are both in good shape."

The doctor looked at him doubtfully, but Hatfield took the vial and the needle. He sterilized the latter in the boiling water, removed it with a pair of forceps and secured it to the barrel of the syringe. Then, while the doctor watched closely, he expertly charged the one-hundredth of a grain dose, lifted the wounded man's arm and drove the needle home, first making sure that no air bubble was present in the barrel.

"Say!" growled the doctor, "where'd you learn to do that? Don't happen to be a surgeon, do you?"

Hatfield smiled slightly and shook his head.

"Well, you handle instruments like one," grunted the doctor. "And you got surgeon's hands, too. Reckon a good one was lost when you took to cow-herding; but then you find all sorts on the rangeland." He peered at the Ranger a moment with his shrewd old eyes.

Hatfield was gazing at the wounded man's face. He lifted his wrist, counted the pulse beats for a minute or more.

"Picking up already," he announced. "And his breathing is easier. I've a notion, suh, that there is no serious brain injury, aside from shock and possible concussion. The blood flow, I noticed when I picked him up, would indicate that."

"Was free, eh?" asked the doctor.

"Decidedly so, and a dark venous blood, at that," Hatfield replied. "Now I guess you'd better take over."

The doctor nodded, growled something under his mustache and went to work. Soon the wound was cleansed and dressed, the injured head swathed in bandages. They got the unconscious man's clothes off and put him in bed. His breathing was easier and there was a slight tinge of color in his pallid face.

"Ought to do now," Hatfield remarked; "and if we can only stave off pneumonia maybe we can save him."

Doctor Beard shot him another keen glance but did not comment. Instead he observed, "Now suppose you tell me what happened?"

Hatfield told him in terse sentences. Beard swore a stream of crackling profanity.

"So it was those hellions I patched up who did it," he said. "If I'd knowed it at the time, I'd have took a chance and reached for my buffalo gun, even though they never took their eyes off me and each one had hold of a hogleg butt all the time. Salty-looking sidewinders."

"I saw five riding down the trail," Hatfield remarked.

"Only two came in," said the doctor. "Might have been others outside with the horses. Reckon they pulled up a piece down the street or in one of the alleys. I don't rec'lect hearing any hoofs. Those two just walked through the door and told me to get to work on them. Didn't figure it was wise to argue. They looked pretty sick but knew what they were doing.

You don't ask questions too much in this section, anyhow."

Hatfield nodded. "You've got something there," he admitted. "You mentioned this man's name—Bill Carter, I believe you said. Who and what is he?"

"Biggest cowman in the section," the doctor replied. "Owns the Cross C. Fine feller, too. I've knowed him for years."

"Nothing off-color against him, then?"

"Hell, no!" snorted Beard. "He's a square-shooter if there ever was one. Salty, sure. You have to be to get ahead in this section. But plumb honest in every respect. And as I said, a fine feller."

"Wonder who would be out gunning for a man like that?" Hatfield said. "It wasn't just a casual shooting. They were chasing him hell-bent-for-leather when I first sighted them."

The doctor seemed to hesitate. "Bill has been bucking the owlhoot organization in this section," he said at length. "Reckon some of 'em were out to even up the score."

"Owlhoot organization?"

"Uh-huh. Been building up for the past couple of years, and of late been getting worse. They've just about taken over the section all the way from Pecos down here and clean to the Rio Grande. Sort of like the old days when Hardin and Kingfisher and Jack Richardson were riding here. Some folks figure they're back again."

"Everybody knows that Hardin and Kingfisher are dead," Hatfield interposed. "And it was pretty well decided that Richardson got his, too, when Kingfisher was killed over at San Antonio."

"Uh-huh, so they say," Doc Beard agreed dryly. "But anyhow, it's like it was before the Rangers busted up the big outlaw outfits and brought something like law west of the Pecos. Rangers have been mighty busy of late, what with the trouble along the Border west of here and those ruckuses down around Laredo and Brownsville, and up in the Panhandle. Haven't had much time for this section and the outlaws have taken advantage of it to get organized again. Lots of folks have written letters to Bill McDowell asking for Rangers to be sent here, but ain't nothing come of it so far."

Hatfield nodded. He did not see fit at the moment to reveal that it was the receipt of those same letters that had caused the salty old Commander of the Border Battalion to send his ace-man.

Hatfield rolled and lighted a cigarette. "That could explain the attack on Carter," he admitted. "Carter hasn't any personal enemies, then?"

Again the old doctor hesitated, longer than before. He shot Hatfield a shrewd and questioning glance.

"I sort of got mixed up in this thing, and I think I ought to know who to look out for," Hatfield suggested mildly.

"Yes, I guess you're right there," Beard agreed. "But Carter hasn't any real enemies that I know of, that is, unless you might figure Tom Kane one."

"Tom Kane?"

"Uh-huh, one of the Kane twins, Tom and Jed."

"And why would Tom Kane have it in for Carter?" Hatfield asked.

"Well, there are a couple of reasons, I reckon," Beard said. "For one thing, Tom Kane got hold of a stretch of land Carter and the other big ranchers always considered open range."

Hatfield nodded his understanding. That could cause plenty of friction. Bloody range wars had been fought over just such incidents.

"And to make matters worse," added Beard, "Kane run sheep critters onto his southwest pastures."

Hatfield's brow drew together. That could be even more serious. He was about to question the doctor more closely when Beard suddenly cocked his head in an attitude of listening. "Folks coming this way," he said. "Sounds like quite a bunch. In a hurry, too. Now what the hell?"

A moment later the door banged open and nearly a dozen men crowded their way into the room. Leading was a very tall man, almost as tall as Hatfield though not so broad-shouldered. He had a questioning gray eye, a hawk nose and a hard mouth. His coat swung back to reveal a small nickel badge pinned to his shirt front.

"What happened, Doc?" he asked, shooting a keen glance at Hatfield. "We heard some feller brought Bill Carter in here shot to pieces."

The old doctor grunted. "Reckon that's so, Walt," he said. "He's badly hurt and if it hadn't been for this feller Hatfield here, I reckon he'd have taken the Big Jump. I'll tell you about it. But the rest of you fellers trail your twine out of here. Carter's in a bad way, and all this gab and thumpin' around can be done without. Clear out now and tell folks not to come stompin' and talking in front of my place. Carter needs quiet. Get going!"

It was evident that Doc Beard's opinions packed considerable weight. The crowd tiptoed out, speaking in whispers. Their boot-heels clicked off along the board sidewalk. Doc shut the door with a growl and turned to the tall man.

"All right, Walt," he said. "Now we'll talk to you. Hatfield I want you to know Walt Nance, the town marshal. Tell Walt what you told me."

Hatfield repeated his story. The marshal listened attentively, fingering his chin.

"Think you'd know any of those fellers if you saw them again?" he asked.

"Sort of doubtful," Hatfield admitted. "Quite a ways across the river up there and the light wasn't too good. One was tall and wide across the shoulders. Another was mighty hefty, but that's about all I could say."

"I see," the marshal said thoughtfully. "There ain't

much doubt about it but the pair Doc patched up belonged to the outfit. You say they rode off, Doc?"

"I didn't say, 'cause I don't know," answered Beard. "They slid out the door after I was finished with 'em. I didn't hear no horses, but they didn't have to have 'em hitched in front of the office. Ain't likely that a couple of hellions in cowhand clothes would be doing much walking. I'd say they hightailed it out of town pronto. Would hardly hang around in the shape they were. Somebody would be sure to notice and ask questions. And remember, they knew somebody on the far side of the river had seen 'em. Likely they'd figure that that somebody was headed for town."

"Yep, the chances are they trailed their twine, and the rest of the bunch with them," Nance said, "But I'll scout around town a bit and see if anybody got a look at 'em." He turned to Hatfield. "Thanks for bringing Bill in, feller," he said. "Reckon he would have been a goner if you hadn't, instead of having a chance to pull through. Say you snaked him up with a rope? Must have been considerable of a chore. Don't see how you managed to do it."

"My horse helped a mite," Hatfield replied with a smile. "If I hadn't had him to tie onto and been able to depend on him, I reckon I couldn't have done it."

The marshal nodded again. "That's him standing outside, ain't it?" he asked. "He's some cayuse, all right. Never saw a finer-looking one. I'm partial to sorrels. Owned one once myself. I just glanced at him as I came in. Mind if I look him over when I go out?"

"Go ahead," Hatfield acceded. "He's friendly enough, but don't try to take hold of the reins or the bit iron. He'll shy away if you do and if you try it again he might chaw your arm a mite."

"I like that sort," said the marshal, "a one-man horse. Sorrels are usually that way, I've noticed, and plumb smart. I won't touch him. Be seeing you later, Doc. I reckon I'll see you again, Hatfield?"

"That's right," the Lone Wolf replied. "I aim to stick around for a day or two, anyhow."

"A good notion," agreed the marshal. "I'll notify Sheriff Blake over to the county seat about what happened. Chances are he'll want to talk to you, seeing as you were the only feller who saw Carter shot."

With a nod he walked out, closing the door behind him. Hatfield turned to Doc Beard, who was putting away his instruments. Doc started to speak, changed whatever he had to say to a yelped curse as a bellow of gunfire sounded outside the office.

4.

HATFIELD BOUNDED ACROSS THE ROOM and flung open the door. For an instant he was outlined clearly against the light within. As he darted out a startled voice yelled—

"Look out! *That's* him!"

Hatfield hurled himself to the side against the wall as red flashes spurted through the gloom. Lead stormed past him, thudding against the wall and fanning his face. His hands streaked to his guns and he sent bullets hissing toward three shadowy shapes on horseback less than a dozen feet down the street. A howl of pain echoed the shots. An answering volley showered him with splinters from the wall. Then the three horses and their cursing riders dashed into the mouth of a dark alley and vanished from sight.

Hatfield raced to the alley and sent three shots whining into the darkness. His ears, ringing from the booming of his own guns, heard hoofs pounding away. The sound ceased abruptly as the unseen riders whisked into an alley between two buildings.

Without taking time to investigate the results of his shots, Hatfield ran back to where the marshal lay on the sidewalk groaning and cursing and thrashing about.

"Leg and arm," he gasped as Hatfield bent over him. "Not bad, I reckon, but hurts like hell."

Old Doc Beard came storming out the door bellowing profanity, a Sharpe's buffalo gun cocked in his hands.

"Where are the damn skunks?" he roared, waving the Sharpe's.

"Got away," Hatfield answered tersely. "Put the hammer down on that darned thing before you blow the town off the map. And give me a hand with the marshal. He's hit."

Beard dropped the gun and joined Hatfield beside the groaning peace officer.

"No bones busted," he grunted after a swift examination. "But that leg's bleeding bad. Help me get him inside."

Shouldering Doc aside, Hatfield picked up the marshal's heavy form as if he were a child and carried him into the office.

"Lay him on that table over there," directed Beard. "Okay. Now help me haul his britches off first thing. Got to get that bleeding stopped."

"Get out of here!" he roared at a man who stuck his excited face in the door at that moment. "And keep everybody else out," he added as feet pounded the board sidewalk. "I got work to do. Shut that door!"

The face vanished and Doc went to work on the marshal. Ten minutes later the bleeding was stanched and the arm and leg were bound up in bandages. Walt Nance, as comfortable as he could be, dragged deep on the cigarette Hatfield had rolled for him.

"I don't know what the hell happened," he replied to Hatfield's question. "I'd just walked over to your horse when the shooting cut loose. Felt like my arm and leg were plumb knocked off. I hit the ground pronto. Your horse scooted across the street. No, I don't think he got hit. Stopped the other side of the street. Then it seemed everybody was shooting in every direction. Did you get any of the sidewinders?"

"Heard one yelp, but he stuck in the hull," Hatfield replied.

"It was the bunch that gunned Carter. I'll bet my last peso on that," the marshal declared and cursed as pain flowed through his wounds.

"Reckon you'd win that bet," Hatfield agreed.

"But why in hell would the buzzards sneak back and drygulch Walt?" demanded the doctor.

"Well," Hatfield replied dryly, "I've a notion the marshal is mighty nigh as tall as myself."

"I'm six-two-and-a-half," grunted Nance. "Reckon maybe you top me by an inch or so."

"About," Hatfield agreed. "Which isn't much difference, and two tall men would look about the same in that dim light out there, especially if they dressed sort of alike."

"Then you figure they were after you!" exclaimed the doctor.

"Reckon so," Hatfield agreed. "When Nance walked up to my horse they naturally figured it was me. They must have been in town all the time and heard about me bringing in Carter. And it appears they don't hanker to have any witnesses to the shooting up the river."

"They holed up in that alley and waited for you to come out," concluded the marshal. "The nerve of them horn toads! Hatfield, it sort of looks like you're a marked man. I reckon the best thing for you to do is ride and ride fast."

Hatfield smiled slightly. "Reckon I'll stick around and have that talk with the sheriff," he said. "Right now I'm going to take a look at my horse."

"Be careful," warned the marshal. "I wouldn't put

it past those devils to come back for another try."

"Reckon they'd hardly have that much nerve," Hat-field replied.

"Not unless one of those fellers happened to be Jack Richardson," said the marshal, tenderly moving his wounded arm to an easier position.

"Jack Richardson!" Hatfield repeated. "What the hell!"

"The big pack leader of the owlhoots of the Pecos River country, and that's saying plenty," growled the marshal.

"Jack Richardson," Hatfield repeated again. "There was a notorious outlaw by that name once, but he was killed."

"Maybe," grunted the marshal. "But plenty of folks will tell you he wasn't killed—that he's alive and kicking right in this section. Tell him about the notes, Doc. You talk better'n I do."

Beard nodded agreement but first tiptoed into the other room to see how Carter was making out. Hatfield took advantage of the opportunity to find Goldy. He glanced keenly about as he passed through the door although he put small stock in the marshal's warning. As he anticipated, groups of men had gathered in the street to discuss the shootings.

"Nance is gunned up a bit, but nothing overly serious, according to what Doc says," he replied to the questions shot at him. "Can't say about Carter. He hasn't recovered consciousness yet, but he's breathing easier and his heart appears to be holding out all right. Beard thinks he should come out of it by morning, but he's going to send for another doctor to make sure there's no serious brain injury."

"That must be Doc Dickinson over to the Del Rio Hospital," hazarded one of the questioners. "Understand he's tops at brain hurts."

Goldy had returned unharmed to his post in front of the building.

"Going to look after *you* in a jiffy," Hatfield promised. "I'll find you a stall and a nosebag. Take it easy for a bit and I'll be with you."

The sorrel's reply was a disgusted snort. Hatfield chuckled and returned to the office. He glanced expectantly at Doc Beard who was filling his pipe.

"As I reckon you've heard, Jack Richardson worked with Kingfisher and Ben and Bill Thompson when they were about the biggest owlhoots in the Southwest," Doc said. "After Kingfisher and the Thompsons were killed, or so the story goes, Richardson drifted down into Mexico and sort of kept under cover for a while. Next he showed up in Arizona."

"I've heard that yarn," Hatfield nodded. "I don't know whether it's true or not. It was never definitely proven that Richardson was killed along with Kingfisher and the Thompson brothers, but folks who should know insisted he·was."

"Maybe," admitted Doc, "but there's a jigger operating in this section who goes by the name of Richardson."

"And the notes Nance mentioned?" Hatfield prompted.

"Every now and then some feller who's found murdered and robbed has a note alongside him," Doc said impressively. "And those notes usually read, '*With the compliments of Jack Richardson*'. And quite a few times some feller who's been talking big against outlaws or been over-active in trying to run 'em down has gotten a draw or drag note signed '*Jack Richardson*'. And if that feller didn't tighten the latigo on his jaw and start 'tending strictly to his own business, he didn't live over-long."

"Sort of throwing down the gauntlet against law and order," Hatfield commented.

"Guess that's about it," Doc nodded. "Anyhow, it's sure got folks hereabouts bad scared. And if you'll rec'lect, Jack Richardson used to write notes like that to folks who'd gotten him on the prod."

"But it's an old owlhoot trick—to take the name of a notorious outlaw," Hatfield said. "To take his name and cash in on his reputation. Jack Richardson was one of the fastest gunhands in all Texas. A man going up against this hellion you've been talking about, believing him to be Jack Richardson, is half whipped at the start. Chances are the yarn about this feller being the original Jack Richardson is just so much malarkey. Notorious killers have a habit of coming to life in folks' imaginations. If all the John Wesley Hardins, Curly Bill Brociuses, and Buckskin Frank Leslies folks have reported seeing from time to time really existed it would take a regiment of cavalry to run 'em down! The really important part of the whole story is that a man who calls himself Jack Richardson is operating in this section. If he's the gent who pulled that stunt tonight he's somebody to reckon with. That was a fine example of cold nerve and fast thinking."

The doctor and the marshal both nodded emphatic agreement. Hatfield sat silent a moment.

"You say this Richardson has a habit of sending a warning note to his intended victim?" he suddenly remarked. "Doc, did you happen to look through Carter's clothes? No? Might be a good notion to do so."

Muttering behind his whiskers, Beard stumped across the room and began rummaging through the wounded rancher's garments. He unearthed a miscellany of articles he carefully laid aside and was about to give up the search when from an overlooked vest pocket he drew forth a crumpled bit of paper. He smoothed it out, glared at it and passed it to Hatfield without comment. The Lone Wolf's black brows drew together again. But he only nodded and handed the paper to Walt Nance. The marshal swore a blistering oath as he read.

Carter, you invited retaliation; you'll get it.
                    (signed) Jack Richardson.

5.

THE MARSHAL SWORE SOME MORE. "So it *was* Richardson who did for Carter!"

"Sort of looks that way," Hatfield admitted.

"And it looks more than ever to me, feller, that you'd better hightail it out of this section," Nance said. "Richardson is after you now and he won't rest till he gets you. It don't matter a damn whether he's the original Richardson or not."

"You're right about that last part," Hatfield agreed, "but for the first part, I aim to be there at the getting. And that's that! Now where can I find a place to put on the nosebag and get a mite of shut-eye? Was riding most of last night and a little ear pounding would come in handy. Need a place to put up my horse, too."

Doc Beard reached for his hat. "If you'll just stay here with Walt for a little while, I'll look after you," he said. "I aim to amble out and round up a few fellers to pack him over to his place. No reason why he can't be moved and he'll be more comfortable there in his bed than stretched out on that hard table. While I'm at it I'll stop at the railroad telegraph office and send a wire to Dickson in Del Rio. He's a top-hand at brain injuries and I want him to look at Carter. Can't never tell about a head wound. From the way the slug went in and come out, I'd say the brain wasn't touched, but I can't be sure."

Hatfield nodded agreement. "I'd say he owes his life to a freak of chance," he commented. "He must have

29

turned in his saddle to look back when the slug hit him. Otherwise it would have gotten him in the back of the head and blown most of it off."

"That's right," Beard nodded. "I hadn't thought of that. Don't miss much, do you?"

Hatfield smiled but didn't reply. Doc Beard headed for the door.

"Now who the hell?" he exclaimed in exasperated tones as fast steps sounded outside. Before he could reach the door it was flung open and a man strode into the office, a tall, well set-up man with a regularly featured face, dark hair, and keen looking eyes back of slightly tinted, thick-lensed glasses.

"Who . . . oh, hello, Brant." exclaimed Beard.

"Where's Carter?" the other asked anxiously. "I just got in town—heard he was killed."

"He ain't," replied Beard, "but he had a mighty close call. If it hadn't been for Hatfield here, he would have been done in, instead of having a good chance to pull through. Hatfield, I want you to know Wilson Brant, Bill Carter's next-door neighbor and a close friend of his."

Brant favored the Ranger with a quick, searching glance. His smile was pleasant, however, and he shook hands with a firm grip.

"Mighty glad to know you," he said. "And if you saved Carter's life, I sure want to thank you for what you did. Fellows over at the Rocking Chair saloon said the whole top of his head was blown off and he didn't have a chance."

"Those terrapin-brained guzzlers are always handing out a lot of sheep dip," grunted Doc. "Take a look at him—you'll see he's a long way from taking the Big Jump."

Brant tiptoed over to the bed and gazed at Carter. He came back shaking his head.

"Poor Bill," he muttered. "He never did anybody any harm that didn't have it coming. Hey—what hap-

pened to you, Nance?" he asked, gazing at the marshal's bandaged members.

"Come along with me to the telegraph office and I'll
tell you about it," interrupted Doc. "I won't be long,
Hatfield," he told the Ranger. "And there's ham 'n eggs
in the kitchen if you care to throw together a surroun-
din'. And a full pot of coffee on the stove all ready to
be heated. Maybe Walt would like a cup."

"Would be prime," Nance said and swore peevishly
as a slight movement sent a twinge through his
wounds.

"Not that I'm complaining," he hastened to assure
Hatfield as the door closed behind Doc and Brant. "If
one of those slugs had hit a bone I'd have stood a good
chance of being a cripple for life. A clean hole heals
fast, so I reckon I haven't anything to kick about."

"Wilson Brant's a nice feller," he continued, as Hatfield busied himself at the stove. "Him and Bill Carter
are good friends. He showed up here about two years
back. Came from the Nueces country, I understand.
Said he'd got fed up with droughts and heat and decided to move. Hung around here in town for a spell
without mentioning his business till he got the lowdown on the section. Then he went straight to Bill
Carter and asked him if it would be okay for him to
take up land here. Carter liked him first off, I guess.
The Rocking R outfit, to the northwest of Carter's
Cross C was up for sale. Old Phil Rader who owned
it had died the year before and his widow wanted to
go back to her folks in Kentucky. Understand Carter
figured to buy in, but after Brant talked with him he
stepped aside and let Brant buy. Brant run his herd
here from over east and brought in his own hands.
First rate cowman. Built up the spread and gets along
fine with everybody, even with Tom Kane who's got
most everybody in the section riled up. He bought what
was always considered open range from the state you
know, and run in sheep critters. Brant says Tom ain't

so bad and would most likely be okay if folks would
just give him a chance. He even persuaded Jed Kane
to speak to Tom now and then."

"Believe Beard mentioned the Kanes are twins,"
Hatfield remarked as he turned the slices of bacon in
the frying pan.

"That's right," said Nance. "You can hardly tell 'em
apart, so far as looks go. Ain't got much else in common, though."

"How's that?"

"Well, it's a long story," said the marshal, "but I'll
hand it to you short. Jed Kane has always been a
steady-going feller, Tom just the opposite. He drank
considerable, liked to gamble, too much in fact, and
was always considerable of a hell-raiser. When their
dad, old Radford Kane, died, they came into the
Slash K spread up to the north of Carter's holdings
and a bit to the West. Brant's Rocking R, incidentally,
is to the west of the Cross C. Well, Jed always saved
his money, Tom spent his. And they never got along
well together. So Jed put it up to Tom, buy or sell.
Tom didn't have anything to buy with. So he said,
'Okay, I'll sell'. Jed bought him out. Tom raised hell
around the section for a while, spending money, and
so forth. Reckon he was just about busted when he
pulled out of the section. Nobody heard a thing about
him for close to ten years. That is, nothing for sure.
Some funny stories came back about him. Said he'd
killed a man in Arizona, then that he was dealing cards
in a place over around San Antonio, and that he got
in trouble over there and hightailed it to Mexico for
a while. Mind you I ain't saying any of all this is true.
You know how such yarns start and how they grow.
Then for a while nothing was heard of him. And then,
about two years ago, he showed up here again. Seemed
to have changed considerable. Used to be a flashy
dresser and, as I said, a free-spender. He'd got a lot
quieter, looked a hell of a sight harder, though he

never was particularly tame. Folks wondered why he'd come back. Then all of a sudden they found out. He'd bought up a big section of what had always been considered open range. First he run in considerable cattle, good-looking cows, too. He brought a bunch of salty hands from somewhere and set up in business. Naturally the oldtimers didn't like it. They'd always considered that section open range."

"Kane got his title from the state?" Hatfield asked.

"That's right. Plumb solid."

"And," remarked Hatfield, "the chances are the oldtimers got to wondering about their own titles. Often they're a might shaky."

"That's right," admitted Nance. "They're always claiming more than they really hold. Reckon it sort of give them a jolt when a feller came in and grabbed off land they'd always considered theirs to do what they wanted to with."

"And got to worrying about who might come along next and grab off a chunk," Hatfield observed.

"Right again. There was some fast scuffling around to make sure about holdings. Well, as I said, that sort of got Tom Kane off on the wrong foot here. Not that he seemed to give a damn. Doesn't seem to have any use for anybody and doesn't care what folks think. Wouldn't have run in sheep critters otherwise, knowing how cow country feels about sheep. All his north range—it runs along the Pecos River and over here to town and clean up to the Cross C—is hills and rocks and brush. Not much good for cows, but the sheep critters seem to make out all right. To the south his holding widens out to the west and is first rate cattle range. That's where he herds his cows. Up to the north, his own stock. And naturally the cowmen are scared for their range with sheep so close by. Everybody knows what sheep do to cattle-grazing land, and when one bunch of sheep shows in a section, it's damn likely more will follow, and there's a lot of open range hereabouts. And once sheep start coming, cows are in for a tough time."

"You're right about that," Hatfield admitted. "The old saying is that sheep can lose every battle and still win the war. And there have been plenty of wars fought because of sheep."

The marshal nodded as he accepted a plate of bacon and eggs and a cup of coffee.

"So naturally folks hereabouts don't think over well of Tom Kane," he added between mouthfuls. "And when things are that way, funny yarns get started about a feller. I'm telling you all this so you won't get the wrong slant on Tom Kane from what you're likely to hear if you coil your twine in this section for a spell —which you shouldn't do with the Richardson bunch on the prod against you. I'm a peace officer and don't take sides. If I catch Tom Kane in any hellishness I'll drop a loop on him quick as the next one, but until I do, he ain't no different in my book from anybody else."

Hatfield nodded. He'd already decided that the marshal was a square man who wouldn't deal in any stray gossip about Tom Kane. It could wait anyway. He'd get the lowdown sooner or later, and he had already had an interesting slant on conditions in the turbulent section.

Hatfield balanced his full plate on his knees and placed a cup of coffee on a convenient chair. A period of busy silence ensued. Finally the marshal, who had managed to assume a sitting position while he ate, handed his empty plate to the Ranger and eased back on the table with a sigh of contentment.

"That helped a hell of a lot," he said. "I was feeling as empty as if I'd leaked out all my vittles through these damn bullet holes."

"You lost a good deal of blood and that's apt to make a fellow feel a mite lank," Hatfield reminded him. "I'll take a look at Carter."

He studied the rancher's face for some moments and listened to his breathing.

"Well?" Nance asked.

"Well, I think he's sound asleep and should wake up his own rational self," Hatfield replied. "I don't believe Doc need worry much about a serious brain injury, though of course we'll have to leave that to the specialist."

"That's good hearing," said the marshal. "Carter is a fine fellow and a good citizen. I'd hate to think of him passing on."

"Don't think he will this time," Hatfield predicted cheerfully as he began cleaning up the kitchen.

Doc Beard reappeared accompanied by four husky men. His first thought was for his patient and he quickly substantiated Hatfield's diagnosis.

"Believe he's going to make out okay, thanks to you, Hatfield," he said. "Well, I wired Dickson over to Del Rio and he'll get here on the morning train. Wired the sheriff, too, while I was about it. Okay, you fellers, haul that stretcher out from under the bed and load Walt onto it. Careful, now, and don't start that bleeding again. Pack him over to his place and put him to bed. I'll drop in a little later. Sam, you hustle right back and sit with Carter while I'm out. I won't be gone more than half an hour at the most."

"Okay, Doc," one of the stretcher-bearers nodded. "Won't take us but a couple of minutes to get over there and back. You go right ahead."

Doc nodded. "Now, Hatfield, come along and I'll lead you to a stable and someplace where you can pound your ear."

Suitable accommodations were quickly found for Goldy. Hatfield left him in the care of an old stable-keeper with bristling white whiskers, a belligerent eye and a sawed-off shotgun.

"Be right here when you want him, cowboy," he assured the Lone Wolf. "This scattergun says so, and

she speaks damn loud." He cocked and uncocked the
old cannon as he spoke. Doc dodged out of the line of
the yawning, twin ten-gauges and expressed his opinion of the stable-keeper in language that smoked. The
keeper replied in kind and both apparently felt better.

"Sorry you had to wait," Hatfield told the sorrel,
"but I don't often get a chance to eat first."

Goldy rolled a disapproving eye in answer and ad-
dressed himself to his feed box.

"Now we'll amble over to the Rocking Chair saloon,"
said Doc. "They got rooms on the second floor and it's
a clean place, upstairs and down. I figure I can stand
a snort about now and we have to go to the bar to sign
up for a room anyhow."

The big room was crowded. Men turned to gaze at
Hatfield with frank interest as he signed the register at
the far end of the bar. Doc answered the questions
about Carter and Walt Nance that were flung at him
and then led the way to a table where they could enjoy
their drink in comfort. Hatfield ran his eyes over the
crowd and decided it was a typical rangeland gathering. Several of the drinkers at the bar and the tables,
he decided were ranch-owners. The majority of the
patrons, however, were punchers.

Several of the owners came over and shook hands
with Hatfield, complimenting him on doing a good
chore.

"You won't have any trouble tying onto a good job
of riding if you figure to stick around," Doc told him.
"Them fellers are all spread-owners. The one that did
the cussin' and said you ought to be in the sheriff's
office is old John Gaylord. Next to Bill Carter he's the
biggest owner in the section. His spread is directly
north of Carter's Cross C."

They were enjoying their second round of drinks
when the swinging doors flew back and a man entered. He was a tall, lean, broad-shouldered man with
an assured almost aggressive bearing. He had dark

hair, a bronze, high-nosed face that was more than passably good-looking and flashing black eyes that seemed to take in the whole room with their quick, glittering sweep. Hatfield felt that there was not a man present he didn't note and mark. He wore two guns slung very low, the butts flaring outward.

"And I'd say he doesn't wear them for ornamental purposes," the Ranger decided.

As the man walked to the bar, a hush fell over the room for a moment, and when the hum of conversation resumed, it was a note or two lower.

The newcomer gave his order in a terse voice. The silent bartender poured a double whiskey into a tall glass. The man downed the fiery liquor at a gulp, as if it had been so much water, and turned and walked out.

"Who was that?" Hatfield asked. " 'Peared to be considerable of a gent."

"That," said Doc very deliberately, "was Tom Kane!"

6.

HATFIELD ROLLED AND LIGHTED a cigarette before speaking again.

"Seemed to sort of throw a spell over the place when he came in," he observed at length. "Everybody shut up for a second."

"Not surprising," Doc replied grimly. " 'Peared like he was looking for somebody, and when Tom Kane is looking for someone, it's likely to be unpleasant.

Reckon everybody wanted to be sure he wasn't the one."

"Sets up to be a salty gent, eh?"

Doc shook his head. "He don't *set up* to be. He *is!* And he's riled quite a few folks considerably since he came back here. Not exactly popular in the section. Not that he gives a hoot. Tom Kane 'pears to thrive on not being popular. Sort of got off on the wrong foot in the beginning and has kept it up. Oh, hell! you'll hear it sooner or later if you stick around, so I might as well be the first to tell you. Mind, though, I don't subscribe to it. Plenty of folks will tell you that Tom Kane is Jack Richardson."

Hatfield said nothing. He studied Doc through the blue mist of his cigarette.

"Do they have any proof to back up the accusation?" he finally asked.

"Nope, but that don't keep 'em from talking."

"Well, what have they got to go on?"

"Not a great deal," Doc admitted, "but what they have got is enough to start blabber-mouths talking. The few folks who've gotten anything like a look at Richardson and lived to talk about it, agree that he's a big, tall, dark-haired gent with dark eyes and wears two guns hung low and to the front."

"That's a description that could fit quite a few folks," Hatfield interpolated.

Doc Beard nodded.

"Then they point out that Kane was around the San Antonio country when Richardson was swaller-forkin' over that section. Some will say that Richardson's description is the same as Tom Kane's plus a mustache and whiskers. And Kane and Richardson showed up missing from San Antonio at just about the same time. Everything was comparatively peaceful hereabouts till Kane showed up two years ago. And they do say that Kane was always a flashy dresser, a gambler and a drinker when he was younger, before he went away. Same description applied to Richardson."

"All of which," Hatfield smiled, "builds up to Jack Richardson come to life in the person of Tom Kane. Interesting, but not very conclusive."

"That's so," admitted the doctor, "but some folks believe it. And Kane hasn't helped any by his high-handed methods of ignoring people's feelings and prejudices. There's been some talk of running him out of the section, but Tom Kane doesn't run easy, and he's got as salty a bunch of jiggers working for him as you ever laid eyes on. Something is likely to bust loose sooner or later, though. I'm mighty glad Bill Carter doesn't appear to be hurt overly bad. That could have easily set the fuse to the powder."

Hatfield nodded thoughtfully and puffed on his cigarette. "Who was it saw Kane over around San Antonio?" he asked suddenly.

"Damned if I know," admitted Doc. "The story just started going around."

"While Kane was over there?"

"Nope. After he came back here. Seems somebody remembered seeing him over there. I really don't know who."

"I see," Hatfield remarked thoughtfully. "By the way, I'd like to have another look at that note you took from Carter's clothes."

"I ain't got it with me," said Doc. "I left it laying on the table. Well, I think I'll be ambling. Don't want to leave Carter too long. And Sam Whitlock will be wanting to get back to his poker game."

"I'll walk over with you," Hatfield said. "I want to see that note."

They left the saloon and headed for Beard's office.

"Now why did that loco hellion put out the light?" Doc said as they approached the building. "And damned if he didn't leave the door half open too. Carter shouldn't have that draft pouring over him."

They had reached the office and were mounting the steps when Hatfield, with a lightning-swift gesture, hurled Doc to one side. In doing so he lost his footing and pitched sideways just as a stream of gun-fire gushed from the dark room.

Quickly regaining his balance, he bounded through the door, gun in hand.

From the rear of the room came the sound of crackling glass. Groping through the darkness, Hatfield made his way to the window while Doc Beard, following in the Ranger's footsteps, stopped long enough to strike a match.

The first thing the flicker of flame showed was a body sprawled on the floor.

"Good God!" exclaimed Beard. "It's Sam Whitlock!"

Convinced that the gunman had made his getaway, Hatfield holstered his gun.

"Wait till I light the lamp," he said quietly. He touched a match to the lamp wick and a soft glow filled the room, outlining the stark form of Whitlock and the body of Bill Carter on the bed, with the handle of a knife protruding from his breast.

7.

ACCUSTOMED AS HE WAS TO SCENES OF VIOLENCE, the old doctor was badly shaken. "Good God!" he repeated over and over.

"Made a clean sweep all right," the Ranger said grimly. "And if I hadn't seen the beam from the street light glint on that hellion's gun as he shifted it, he'd likely have added one or both of us to his tally."

Doc swabbed at the sweat streaming down his face.

"I reckon if you hadn't taken time to shove me out of the way, it would have been me for sure," he said.

"Lucky for me I did," Hatfield deprecated. "I lost my balance at just the right second. Well, guess you might as well send another telegram to Doctor Dickson at Del Rio that his services won't be needed. And send another one to the sheriff telling him that his certainly are. We've got a double murder on our hands."

"But, my God! What does it all mean?" panted the old doctor. "Why did they come back and kill Carter? Why would they take such a chance?"

"I think," Hatfield replied quietly, "because Carter knew who shot him there by the river." He reached down and brushed his hand across the seat of the chair beside the table as he spoke.

"Makes sense," Beard agreed, giving Hatfield a quick look. "And *you* saw him shot," he added significantly. "Look out! Somebody's comin'."

Hatfield had already heard the steps approaching, but they were too swift and purposeful to cause him alarm.

"The shot must have been heard," he said. "Somebody's coming to see what happened."

A moment later two punchers stuck their heads in the half-open door.

"More trouble, Doc?"

"Plenty," Beard replied heavily. "Preston, run across to Walt Nance's place and tell him everything's under control. He must have heard the shot, too, and he's likely to come crawling over here on his one good leg. Bates, you hustle to the Rocking Chair and get John Gaylord and Hilary Austin if they're still there. And try and find Wilson Brant. He may be down at the Ace-Full."

When the pair had hurried away on their errands, Beard knelt beside the body of Whitlock.

"Was a powerful hellion that hit him," he muttered. "Skull smashed like an eggshell. Used a gun barrel, I'd say. Must have slipped up behind him."

"Don't think so," Hatfield replied.

Doc glanced over his shoulder. "Why?"

"Because," Hatfield said, "the chair Whitlock was sitting in is still warm, and the chair faces the door. He was hit after he stood up and turned around. Whoever did it came in the front door. If he'd come in through the back he would have run out that way and not gone through the window."

"That's right," Doc agreed. "The back door is always locked. Say! you sure don't miss much, as I said before. And you figure Whitlock knew whoever came in the door?"

"Knew him and had no reason to believe he intended any harm," Hatfield replied. "There's no sign of a struggle. I'd say Whitlock turned to look at something to which the killer pointed, perhaps Carter. He was evidently facing the bed when he was struck."

"And then the sidewinder went over to the bed and drove a knife through Carter's heart. Wonder why he blew out the lamp?"

"Either against the chance of some passerby seeing him and recognizing him or he heard us coming this way, which is unlikely," Hatfield said. "He'd hardly hear us before we turned the corner, and the light was out when we first sighted the building. Most likely he blew out the light as soon as he struck Whitlock down. He had to be familiar with the layout of the rooms. He evidently knew just where to go after he fired that shot. I noticed the window he went through is not in line with the inner door. He had to make a turn to reach it and he never hesitated."

Doc turned to peer at the window in question and

as he did so, Hatfield picked up a scrap of paper from the table and deftly slipped it into his pocket.

A crowd had gathered outside. Men pushed into the office, among them the two elderly ranch-owners, Hilary Austin and John Gaylord.

"Wanted you fellers to witness what has happened before anything was moved," Doc Beard told them. "We'll hold an inquest in the morning as soon as Sheriff Thompson gets here."

An ugly mutter ran through the crowd as men stared with hard eyes at the two bodies. Hatfield knew there was the making of a lynching party in that room. A very small spark would set off an explosion of unreasoning violence.

Preston and Wilson Brant made their way to the front of the group.

"Guess it's curtains for poor Bill this time," Doc Beard told him sadly.

Brant walked over to the bed and gazed down at Carter. His face was set in hard, vindictive lines. His eyes gleamed back of his glasses.

"Somebody should stretch rope for this," he said.

"And I got a notion who it should be," said a voice from the crowd.

Brant turned to glance at the speaker. "Bates," he said, "you have no right to make an accusation you can't back."

"He was in town tonight," the other declared stubbornly.

"Because Tom Kane was in town tonight is no proof that he came here and killed Carter," Brant replied.

"Everybody knows there was bad blood between them," insisted Bates.

Again the low, ominous mutter ran through the crowd. Hatfield fervently hoped that Tom Kane had left town. His eyes grew thoughtful as he studied Brant.

"Bad blood engendered by a difference doesn't

necessarily result in a killing," Brant was saying. "I'd say this is the work of the Richardson gang."

"And who the hell is Jack Richardson?" someone shouted.

Old John Gaylord spoke up. "I figure we've had enough loose gabbin'," he said. "Sheriff Thompson will take over in the morning and he's a good conscientious peace officer."

"And behind the door when they were handing out brains," somebody muttered.

But evidently Gaylord packed authority in the section, for the argument was not resumed.

"Somebody will have to break the news to Miss Mary," Doc Beard said.

"I'll do that, but it'll be a tough chore," Wilson Brant volunteered. "And I'll arrange to have Bill's body taken home for burial. I'll ride up there right away."

"She's Carter's daughter—his wife's dead," Doc whispered to Hatfield.

The crowd began to file out. Two men volunteered to stay in the office and see that nothing was disturbed pending arrival of the sheriff.

"Much obliged," Doc told them gratefully. "Then I'll go over to the Rocking Chair and go to bed. I'm all in. Come on, Hatfield, you must be pretty well done up, too."

Hatfield paused long enough to examine the two bodies carefully, noting the location of the wound on Whitlock's head and the position of the knife in Carter's breast. Then with a last glance at the murder scene, they left the office.

"Hatfield," Doc said as they crossed the street, "this thing has all the makings of a first-rate range war."

The Lone Wolf nodded soberly.

"Thank God Carter's Cross C outfit wasn't in town tonight," Doc continued. "They're plenty salty, too. If they had been and had tangled with Kane and his bunch we'd have had a corpse-and-cartridge session for fair. I hope Sheriff Thompson will be able to keep things in hand. But as that feller said tonight, I'm afraid old Rolf Thompson was sort of behind the door when they were handing out brains. He's a tough customer and absolutely a square-shooter, but he doesn't think overly fast. Where cold nerve and a fast gunhand are in order, there's no better along the Border but I'm scared that whoever is back of all this, will keep a jump ahead of Thompson. Why in hell doesn't Bill McDowell send a troop of Rangers down here? He knows what's going on. Must have got a dozen letters from folks down here in the past month. From what I know of McDowell, he isn't the sort to let folks down. Four or five Rangers stationed in this section would put a crimp in the Richardson gang pronto. They'd be scared to operate with Rangers on the job. I don't know what's got into McDowell."

"Understand he's got considerable on his hands and too few men for the various chores," Hatfield observed as they neared the saloon. "And the kind of things that have been happening around here are usually referred to the local authorities. Only when the local peace officers appear to be unable to cope with a situation do the Rangers move in."

"Well, then, it's about time they did a bit of moving," grunted Beard. "Wideloopings! Killings! Hold-ups! Getting to be the regular thing hereabouts. And what's happened already won't be anythin' if a couple of outfits like the Cross C and Kane's Diamond T really tangle."

"Speaking of Kane," Hatfield remarked with apparent irrelevance, "is he an educated man?"

"Oh, he can write his name and add and subtract a bit, if that's what you mean," Doc replied. "Don't think he ever got much schooling. Didn't finish the common school, if I remember right. Dropped out at the third or fourth grade and got him a job of riding, like so many of the cowhand breed. Soon as they learn to count up to forty dollars and sign their name to a receipt, they figure they know enough. Jed Kane did a mite better, though. He finished the grades and had a couple of years in college, I believe. Old Man Kane would have sent Tom along too, if he'd stood for it, but Tom 'lowed he didn't have no time for such high-falutin' foolishness. He went to work."

Hatfield nodded thoughtfully as they entered the saloon.

"We'll stop for one drink and a smoke and then go to bed," Doc suggested, leading the way to a table.

As he listened to snatches of conversation, Hatfield concluded that Doc's fears were not exaggerated. The atmosphere was ominous. He quickly gathered, also, that while the prevailing sentiment was against Tom Kane, it was by no means unanimous. Evidently there were quite a few small owners in the section, some of them doubtless newcomers, who resented the high-handed attitude of the older cattle barons and were inclined to side with anybody who opposed them.

"When anything goes wrong, blame it on a little feller," he heard one truculent individual remark to a companion. "Anything a big owner does is okay, but the little feller is always plumb out of order. Well, we'll see."

"That's part of their game," said the other. "Cover up their own hellishness by yelling that anybody who don't lay claim to a million acres is responsible. Wouldn't be a bit surprised to find out that one of his own bunch of land grabbers did for that Carter feller. One of 'em got an eye on his holdings. Just wait and see who ends up owning the Cross C. Betcha that daughter of Carter's ain't able to hang onto the spread. Just wait and see."

Hatfield became more disturbed with every remark. If real trouble broke out, people would begin taking sides. Soon the section would be divided into two hostile camps. Similar developments had started the terrible Lincoln County war and the other cattle wars that were bloody chapters in rangeland history.

"Looks like I've got my work cut out to bust up this thing before it gets started," he mused. "But I'll be danged if I know where to start. I've learned a couple of interesting things, however. Little things that might turn out to be big things. Okay, Doc, I'm ready to go upstairs if you are."

Tired though he was, Hatfield did not go to bed immediately. First he cleaned and oiled his guns, then he took out the crumpled note he had found on Bill Carter and studied it for some time.

"Rather unusual wording," he mused. *Carter, you invited retaliation; you'll get it.* The punctuation and handwriting were hardly that of the average cow hand. Yes, the whole composition was rather unusual, Hatfield thought.

He replaced the note and rolled a cigarette. For some time he sat smoking and thinking. He picked up one of his guns and squinted through the gleaming barrel.

"Jack Richardson," he remarked to the big six.

Jack Richardson! Hatfield knew that once such characters had departed from the scene, an aura of glamor and romance often gathered about their memory. Richardson, so the story went, was a man of culture, refinement and considerable education. Reckless, splendidly brave, taciturn and aloof, an embittered man who had fled from Virginia because of a killing in which he felt he was justified, he had finally drifted to Texas and taken up with the outlaws of the Southwest although he had little in common with them.

So much for legend. The cold and proven facts concerning the man were grim enough. Richardson had been to the Kingfisher-Thompson-Hardin gang what John Ringo was to the Curly Bill Brocius outlaw organization of Cochise county, Arizona—the brains. He had planned and directed their forays and enabled them to escape punishment for their crimes. John Wesley Hardin, the cold killer, and ferocious Ben Thompson were the leaders in the field, but behind them was the clear, calculating mind of Jack Richardson. When Richardson spoke, even the utterly fearless and utterly merciless Kingfisher listened and obeyed. His companions knew that Richardson was not only more deadly than any of them, he was also more intelligent, resourceful and farseeing. They respected him and, so far as they were capable of such an emotion, they feared him. When Richardson finally broke with them, Kingfisher and the Thompsons quickly became victims of their enemies and Hardin and others were caught in the toils of the law. That much was known. The rest was largely surmise. Some folks contended that Richardson died in the blazing gun-battle that wiped out Kingfisher and the Thompsons. Others declared that Richardson never rejoined his companions once he broke with them, that he merely vanished into obscurity.

"Let's see, now," Hatfield mused, "just how did Captain Hudson describe Richardson in that account he wrote of him? Think it went something like this— Richardson was about twenty-three or four, shortly before he was reported to have been killed. He dressed flashily, rather in the fashion of the gambling fraternity, wore a mustache and a short beard. Also wore his hair rather long, another mark of the professional gambler. Was tall with broad shoulders and deep chest. A powerful man. He was on the dark side—eyes and hair. A dead shot and very fast on the draw. Opinionated, and ready to back up his opinions at all times. Dangerous, cold, calculating. Absolutely without fear and without mercy. Yes," Hatfield said to himself. "That was about it. A shave and a haircut would make a fellow like that look decidedly different. And in the course of six or seven years he might put on weight, which would tend to change his appearance, too."

He loaded his gun and went to bed.

8.

THE FOLLOWING DAY broke hot and still. Hatfield was awakened by Doc Beard tapping on the door. They went down to a late breakfast in their shirtsleeves.

While they were waiting for their order, three men entered the saloon. One was Wilson Brant, the Rocking R owner. A second was a big, burly man with thick, bowed shoulders. His face was blocky and he had cloudy, brown eyes and a tight-lipped mouth that twisted derisively at the corners. For a moment Hatfield thought the third member of the trio was Tom Kane. A second glance, however, told him he was wrong. The man was much the same build as Tom Kane, the same coloring and he was remarkably like him in feature. But his eyes had a quieter look, and his bearing lacked the swagger that marked Tom Kane. Hatfield rightly surmised that he must be Jed Kane, Tom's twin brother. This was corroborated when Doc Beard called to the new arrivals to join them.

"Jed, this is Hatfield, the man who brought in Bill Carter," Wilson Brant said. "Hatfield, I want you to know Jed Kane, and Chuck Taylor, my range boss."

Hatfield acknowledged the introductions and shook hands. The three men sat down at Doc's invitation.

"I ate a bite real early, but I think I can stand a bowl of stew," said Brant after glancing at the scrawled bill of fare.

"I want a drink," grunted the burly Taylor. He got up and slouched to the bar.

"Take it easy, now," Brant called after him. "We've got work to do."

Taylor grumbled something unintelligible and signaled the barkeep.

A moment later a waiter arrived with an armload of dishes. He placed a bowl of steaming stew in front of Wilson Brant. As Brant leaned over to inspect the dish, the rising steam fogged his glasses. With a mutter of irritation he removed them and polished the thick lenses vigorously with a handkerchief, glancing toward the bar as he did so.

"Taylor!" he called preemptorily, "put that bottle down! You know I don't want you drinkin' tequila. You're loco enough as it is without that poison. Put it down, I say! Bartender, give him one shot of whiskey, and that's all."

Taylor glared across the room at his employer and grumbled an oath. But he shoved the fiery Mexican potation aside, gulped the glass of whiskey the bartender poured him and lumbered back to the table, wiping his mouth with the back of his huge, hairy hand. Wilson Brant replaced his glasses and began eating his stew.

Jim Hatfield's black brows drew together thoughtfully but he did not comment on the incident.

They had just finished eating when a lanky old man with a big silver badge pinned to his sagging vest came through the swinging doors and glanced about.

"It's Sheriff Thompson," said Doc. "This way, Rolf."

The sheriff was introduced to Hatfield and shook hands. Doc Beard tersely told him the part the Ranger had played in Bill Carter's rescue. The sheriff nodded approval.

"All set for the inquest?" he asked. "Guess we'd better get busy."

The inquest, held in Doc Beard's crowded office, did not take long. Doc as coroner presided. The verdict of the coroner's jury was brief and to the point: Carter and Whitlock met their death at the hands of parties unknown. The sheriff was advised to run down the varmints as quickly as possible. The inquest adjourned and preparations were made to remove the bodies.

A light wagon drove up to the office. Wilson Brant handled the reins and beside him was a tall, slender girl with hair the color of ripe corn silk and dark blue eyes that were swollen from weeping. Her sweet and extraordinarily pretty face was composed, however. Hatfield liked her looks.

"It's Miss Mary, Bill Carter's daughter," said Doc Beard. "Come along, Hatfield, I want you to meet her."

The Ranger bared his black head and accompanied Doc to the wagon.

"Mary, this is Jim Hatfield who did all he could to save your dad," Doc said. "Reckon Wilson told you about it."

"Yes, he did," replied the girl, extending a slender, sun-golden little hand. "And I want to thank you, Mr. Hatfield. I hope you'll come to the—the funeral."

"I'll be glad to, ma'am," Hatfield replied courteously.

The girl smiled tremulously and a touch of color showed in her pale cheeks.

"Brad Dwyer, our range boss, is in town," she said. "He'll be glad to have you ride with him to the ranchhouse."

Carter's blanket-wrapped body was loaded into the wagon and the horses moved ahead. Chuck Taylor, slouching in his saddle, walked a big bay after the wagon.

"Brant has taken care of everything," Doc told Hatfield. "Must have been a tough chore, telling Mary about what happened to her dad. I think Wilson likes her pretty well."

"A mighty pretty girl," Hatfield observed. "Reckon it isn't hard for any man to like her."

A short, heavy-set man with bristling red hair and

choleric blue eyes approached, glancing questioningly at Hatfield.

"Hello, Brad," said Doc. "Hatfield here will ride to the ranch with you for the funeral. Reckon you heard about him."

"Reckon I did," admitted the other, extending a gnarled fist, "and I ain't likely to forget what he did for the Boss. Glad to know you, Hatfield, mighty glad. I'll be ready to ride in about an hour. That okay?"

"Okay," Hatfield replied as they shook hands.

"I'll meet you here at Doc's office," said Brad Dwyer. "Got a few chores to do, but I won't be long."

He hurried off, swinging his blocky shoulders, his bowed legs twinkling.

"Good man," said Beard. "With Carter for years. Yes, a good cowman, but likely to fly off the handle. Came pretty near taking a shot at Tom Kane last week. Walt Nance stopped it in time. Good thing for Dwyer, I guess. He ain't no slouch with a gun, but Tom Kane always was chain lightning. Funny thing happened just a few days before that. Bill Carter bumped into Kane over to the Rocking Chair. One word led to another and Carter just about put it up to Tom to draw or drag. Everybody thought it was curtains for Carter, but Tom just looked at him a minute, turned his back and walked away. Carter was plumb flabbergasted, and I've a notion, a mite relieved. Bill wasn't scared of anything that walks or creeps, and he was ready to take Kane on, but I've a feeling he didn't figure to live long once he reached."

Hatfield said nothing.

"What did you think of Jed Kane?" Doc asked. "Nice quiet feller, isn't he? Hardly spoke a dozen words while we were eating. Pity Tom isn't more like him. Funny, ain't it, that two fellers who look so much alike are so different in other ways. They never got along. As I told you before, Wilson Brant has been trying to get them together, but I reckon he hasn't had over-much luck."

Hatfield fished out the makin's and rolled a cigarette. "Doesn't Brant ever pack a gun?" he asked, as if the question were irrelevant. "I noticed he didn't have one last night, nor this morning either. Funny for this section."

"Nope, he never does," replied Doc. "Says he's better off without one. His eyes are so bad he can't see to shoot straight, and folks usually won't thrown down on an unarmed man. Guess he's right."

"If a man can't handle a gun, he is better off without one," Hatfield agreed. "Well, I'll go get my horse and wait for Dwyer."

9.

WHEN HATFIELD RETURNED WITH GOLDY, Doc Beard had tidied up the office, the body of Whitlock had been removed. Hatfield went in and waited till Dwyer put in an appearance.

"All ready to go?" he asked the Lone Wolf. Hatfield was, and they rode off together.

Dwyer was a taciturn individual and hardly spoke till they had crossed the rim and were riding up the trail that flanked the Pecos gorge.

"Was it right about here the Boss was done in?" he asked suddenly.

"A little farther on, around the next bend," Hatfield replied. "He was quite a way up the trail when I first spotted him."

"Guess they jumped him while he was crossing Tom Kane's holding," Dwyer growled. "Hatfield, there are folks that shouldn't be allowed to stay alive."

"I agree with you," Hatfield said, "but the question always is, who?"

"Sometimes it ain't so hard to answer," Dwyer returned significantly.

"But one you want to be sure you've got the right answer," Hatfield replied. "Jumping at conclusions is bad business, especially where a life is involved."

Dwyer grumbled under his breath but apparently couldn't find an adequate reply. He was silent for a couple of miles of brushy, rocky terrain. Suddenly his face darkened and he jerked his thumb to the left.

"There're some of the damn woolies that that buzzard Kane brought in to spoil the range," he said.

Hatfield stared at the alert little creatures cropping leaves and twigs from a stand of bluebrush. They had long, tight-locked fleece hanging so low as to almost hide their dainty split hooves. The horns of the bucks were powerful, curving backward and down from their skulls. He turned wonderingly to the glowering Dwyer.

"So those are the critters Kane brought in," he remarked. "Well, I'll be! Dwyer, do you call those things sheep?"

"Sure," the range boss replied, "why not? He's got thousands of them back in them hills."

"The same kind?"

"Uh-huh. Funny-lookin' breed, ain't they?"

"Damn funny!" Hatfield replied. "As it happens, they're not sheep at all."

"Then what the hell are they?" Dwyer demanded.

"Goats!" Hatfield replied, "Angora goats."

"Goats!" Dwyer repeated. "Don't look like any goats I ever saw. And anyhow, what's the difference?"

"One hell of a difference so far as cowmen are concerned," Hatfield replied. "Dwyer, why are cowmen so set against sheep coming onto their range?"

Dwyer stared at the Ranger as if he were convinced that the man had taken leave of his sense. "Because they ruin the range," he snorted. "With their damn chisel hoofs they cut the ground to pieces, and they eat the grass right down to the roots so it won't grow again. A herd of them blattin' woolies can ruin a section of range in no time, and they keep right on moving along and ruining more. Any damn fool knows that!"

"And I suppose a breeder of Angora goats would say that any damn fool should know that Angoras don't do any such thing," Hatfield replied. "I won't say it, however, because Angoras are new over here. I never saw them this far west before. Plenty of them farther east, in Uvalde county and other places."

"Feller, will you please tell me what the hell you're talking about?" begged the bewildered range boss. "What do you mean when you say they won't spoil the grassland?"

"I mean," Hatfield explained patiently, "that Angoras don't eat grass, and they don't graze. They browse. Browse on tender twigs and buds and leaves. In the winter they go for evergreen. Put them out on the open grasslands and they'd starve to death. In kidding time, the ewes will go for a little grass, the kind of grass that's growing between the scattered brush over there, to increase their milk supply. But they don't like it, and they don't make a regular diet of it any more than you'd make a steady diet of castor oil. Angoras must have plenty of brush to survive, the kind of brush those slopes and hills over there are covered with. Look at that mountain mahogany and bluebrush. And there's service, and lots of piñon. Angoras like piñon nuts. Drive a flock of them onto your best pasture and they'd just stand around bleating for something to eat. Tom Kane was smart when he brought Angoras in here. He must have learned considerable about them somewhere and realized this section of his range would be prime for them. He'll make more on them than he does on his cows. Angora fleece and hides are worth plenty. Understand what I'm talking about now?"

Dwyer swore, tugged at an ear, scratched his bristling red head and 'lowed maybe he did.

"What I can't understand," added Hatfield, "is why Kane didn't tell folks about the habits of Angoras when he brought them in, instead of letting them think he was just running in another brand of sheep."

"Guess Kane doesn't tell folks around here anything," Dwyer grunted. "He's been damned uppity ever since he showed back here."

"Or ever since he was jumped for getting title to land that had been considered open range?" Hatfield suggested mildly.

"May be something to that," Dwyer admitted, "but he didn't have no right to do it."

"Why?"

"Because this has always been open range," Dwyer returned belligerently. "There's been too much of that sort of thing going on hereabouts in the past few years. It's got to be put a stop to, and we aim to do it."

Hatfield smiled, a trifle sadly.

"That's where you're wrong, Dwyer," he said earnestly. "You can't stop it. What you call open range is state-owned land and anybody willing to pay for it can get title. The only way the oldtimers, the big owners, can hang onto it is to get title. And they won't, because they don't really need it. The country is filling up and the day of the open range is just about done. Next there'll be wire."

"Barbed wire west of the Pecos?" scoffed Dwyer. "It won't never happen."

"That's what the oldtimers up in the Panhandle and the Trinity River country said," Hatfield countered. "But there are thousands of miles of wire up there now, and more coming all the time. All the big spreads up there are fenced. Why? Because they've learned by experience that it pays. They don't spend thousands of dollars on fence for fun. Fenced range is more economical to work. It removes the need of a round-up and the tedious and expensive chore of cutting out and separating the various brands. Cows behind wire are much easier to handle. An owner just picks up what he needs and shoots them to market. He has his beef to market before the round-up cows are ready to hit the trail. It's happened in other sections, and it'll happen here. The oldtimers can't stop the wheels of progress and they might as well make up their minds to accept changed conditions and get along peaceably with their new neighbors."

"How the hell you going to get along with an owlhoot like Tom Kane?" Dwyer demanded querulously.

"Well," Hatfield responded with a grin, "from what I've been learning, it appears to be something of a chore, all right. Kane is evidently bull-headed as a brindled shorthorn. The way he's handled the goat business proves that. When Carter jumped him about getting title to the land, instead of talking reasonable and pointing out that he was absolutely right, Kane got on his high-horse and did all he could to keep the fires burning. And as a result made trouble for everybody, himself included."

"There are folks who will tell you he's Jack Richardson," Dwyer remarked.

"Any proof that he is?" Hatfield countered.

"Well, if you mean has anybody caught him dead to rights, I reckon the answer is no," Dwyer admitted.

"Exactly," Hatfield said, "and it isn't exactly the American way to prejudge a man on hearsay evidence."

Dwyer flushed a little at the implication. Suddenly he turned in his saddle to face Hatfield.

"Feller, you were closer to what went on than anybody else," he said. "Do you believe he killed the Boss?"

"Dwyer," Hatfield replied slowly, "I don't know

whether Tom Kane killed Carter. I don't know whether you killed him, or Doc Beard, or the sheriff. In other words, I don't know who killed Carter. But," he added grimly, "I figure to find out."

Dwyer regarded the Ranger for a moment. "Got a feeling maybe you will," he admitted. "You 'pear to take considerable interest in the business."

"Well," Hatfield replied dryly, "I've had lead thrown at me three times in the past twenty-four hours. That's likely to cause a man to take an interest in what's going on."

"You got something there," Dwyer agreed, "and I'm telling you for your own good, you can figure to have more thrown at you if you stick around this section. The Boss finally stopped one, but it wasn't the first time he heard it whistle. Ever since he started gunning for Richardson things have happened. A couple of months back the Richardson bunch ran off a shipping herd from our southwest pasture. Killed both night hawks, got a good head start and shoved the cows across the Rio Grande. But the Boss was smart. He was an oldtimer who knew this whole section like he knew the palm of his hand. We lit out after those wide-looping coyotes by way of a short-cut he knew. We caught up with them below the Line and had a nice running fight. Killed two of 'em and got the cows back."

"Nobody recognized the pair as tied up with any outfit up here?"

"Nope," Dwyer replied. "None of us had ever seen 'em before. Nothing outstanding about 'em. Reg'lation brush-popping scum. Then when the owlhoots held up the Pecos stage and got twenty thousand in gold, the Boss got a posse together and lit out after 'em. Trailed 'em into the hills to the southwest and would have caught 'em up if dark and a rainstorm hadn't come to make things worse. Two mornings later we found a note pinned to the ranchhouse door telling the Boss that Richardson was out to get him. He was shot at a couple of times from the brush but he didn't pay it much mind. Then old Sam Childers who had been with the Boss for thirty years and had more to do with running the spread than Bill himself was found dead in the trail, with a Richardson note beside him. And now the Boss has been done in. See what I mean?"

Hatfield nodded thoughtfully, his eyes roving the brush grown hills to the left.

"Does any of this tie up with Tom Kane?" he asked.

Dwyer shook his head. "Nothing definite. Except the night before we found that note on the door a Mexican the Boss had some dealings with saw Kane riding not far from our ranchhouse. And a prospector reported seeing him up close to the *casa* one night, acting as if he was waiting for somebody."

"Could have a legitimate explanation," Hatfield observed, but his mind went back to the fact that just before Bill Carter was knifed to death, Tom Kane had come into the Rocking Chair saloon as if he were looking for somebody.

"Could have been getting a line on Doc and me," he mused to himself. "Making sure the coast was clear. Just surmise, of course, and not overly definite, but there it is. I'd like to have a little talk with *Senor* Kane."

10.

THEY HAD BEEN RIDING STEADILY while they talked and the country was changing. The hills had petered out. The trail veered away from the river and ran across rolling rangeland well-groved and watered and spotted with fat cattle.

"The Cross C holding," said Dwyer, a note of pride in his voice.

"Fine cow country," Hatfield commented. "Don't see why anybody with a holding like this would hanker for that mess of brush and rocks to the south."

"Well, I guess it was just the principle of the thing," Dwyer defended.

"And handled in an unprincipled manner," Hatfield remarked. "Like the dog in the manger who couldn't eat the hay and snapped at the hungry horse."

Dwyer flushed again. "The Boss wasn't that sort of a feller, Hatfield," he said.

"No, not as a person," Hatfield conceded. "But he was representative of a class and a way of thinking that's outmoded."

Dwyer tugged his ear. "You're a funny feller, Hatfield, for a wandering cowpoke," he remarked.

"Perhaps, for a wandering cowpoke," Hatfield agreed with a smile. "Guess that's the Cross C *casa* up there ahead, isn't it?"

"Yep, that's it," Dwyer replied. "Nice layout, don't you think?"

Hatfield did. He eyed the big, white ranchhouse, set in a grove, and the tight outbuildings beyond.

Dwyer wore a worried look. "She's a fine spread," he said, "but I don't know how things will be going from now on. The Boss ran things right up to the hilt, but now I dunno. I know all there is to know about handling range work, but when it comes to the business end, I just ain't up to it, and I admit it."

"How about Carter's daughter?" Hatfield asked.

"She's a fine gal and smart, but she don't know anything about the cow business," Dwyer replied. "You see, up to the first of this year, except for visits, she always lived with Carter's sister over to Houston. Her mother died when she was born, and Carter's sister took her then. When the aunt died last year, she came back to live with her dad. Yes, she's a fine gal. She can ride and shoot, but she never learned anything about ranching. Worked in a bank over to Houston.

"But maybe Wilson Brant will be taking over before long," Dwyer resumed hopefully. "I think he's sort of sweet on her, and he sure knows the cow business. You can't tell about a woman, though. Maybe she likes him, maybe she don't."

"Yes, that might solve the problem," Hatfield admitted thoughtfully.

Dwyer was also looking thoughtful. His brow wrinkled as he laboriously turned something over in his slow mind. "Hatfield," he asked abruptly, "who'd you work for last?"

"The XT," Hatfield answered, with truth.

"That's a big one!" said Dwyer. "Ridin' for them, of course?"

"I was their range boss," Hatfield replied quietly.

Dwyer's eyes widened. "Range boss for the XT!" he repeated. "That must have been considerable of a chore. How come you left 'em?"

"Ever hear about itchy feet?" Hatfield parried the question.

"Reckon I have," Dwyer chuckled. "I sure had 'em when I was younger, about your age. I rode for spreads all over the Southwest. Even got up into Montana once. Didn't like it. Those paper-backed buzzards up there take dallies, instead of tieing hard and fast! I figure if you want to turn something loose you hadn't oughta dropped a loop on it in the first place."

Hatfield chuckled at this ingenious exposition of the age-old controversy between Texans who fasten their ropes securely to the saddle horn, and the punchers of the Northwest who take a couple of turns around the horn but leave the end of the rope free to facilitate a quick release of the twine if they need it.

"So you were range boss for the XT," Dwyer repeated a second time. "Hmmm!" His brow had cleared and he seemed pleased about something.

A few minutes later they rode into the ranchhouse yard. Dwyer let out a bellow and a wrangler came hurrying to take charge of the horses.

In the big living room of the ranchhouse a number of men were assembled, including Wilson Brant, Jed Kane and the two big owners, Gaylord and Austin. Crotchety, wizened old John Gaylord waddled across the room and shook hands with Hatfield.

"By gad, you're a man!" he said. "By gad! I say you are! You're the sort we need around here. Like to have a talk with you. Ride up to my place, the Lazy G, when you find time. Anybody can tell you how to get there. Ride up."

Hatfield accepted the invitation with a smile and Gaylord lumbered off.

"Reckon old John figures to try and talk you into signing up with him," Dwyer chuckled softly to Hatfield. "But I got a notion he'll find he missed his throw."

"Why?" Hatfield asked curiously.

Dwyer grinned and winked. "You'll find out," he replied and would say no more.

After dinner most of the gathering, including Brant and Kane, rode off. Gaylord, Austin and one or two others volunteered to sit up with the dead.

"Mighty glad you saw fit to come," Brant told Hatfield before he left. "Hope you'll see your way clear to staying on in the section. As Gaylord said, we need men like you."

Jed Kane also came over to say good-bye. He appeared to be a pleasant, diffident individual, quite different from his twin brother. Hatfield felt that he deferred to Wilson Brant, who, the Ranger decided, was anything but diffident, though pleasant enough.

"Got a notion he can be hard as nails when necessary, though," the Lone Wolf mused as he gazed after Brant's broad back. "Sure sounded that way when he told that tough-looking range boss of his to put down the bottle of tequila. Noticed Taylor didn't argue with him, either. But I'd sure like to get a look through those glasses he wears."

Brad Dwyer, who had been absent for some time, suddenly reappeared.

"Like to amble down to the bunkhouse and meet the boys?" he suggested.

Hatfield was agreeable and they left the ranchhouse together. When they entered the bunkhouse, which proved to be large, well-fitted up and airy, Hatfield sensed an air of expectancy in the dozen or more hands gathered there. They were of all ages and sizes, having in common an appearance of efficiency, he thought. At the moment they were serious, as was to be expected under the circumstances, but ordinarily they were a rollicking, carefree bunch, ready for anything that promised fun or excitement, a fight, a foot-race or a frolic.

Dwyer rattled off a series of names with bewildering speed, but during the exchange of conversation that followed, Hatfield never failed to address a man by his proper handle.

"What do you think of 'em?" Dwyer asked as they returned to the ranchhouse.

"Look like good men," Hatfield replied. "I've a notion they can be plenty salty should occasion warrant."

"Guess you've got the right notion, only sometimes I got trouble following you," Dwyer said. "You're considerable of an educated feller, ain't you?"

"I went to school, if that's what you mean," Hatfield laughed.

"Uh-huh, considerable, I take it," Dwyer agreed dryly. "You and Wilson Brant ought to get along together prime. Can't understand what he's sayin' half the time, either."

Meanwhile, Hatfield was the subject of animated discussion in the bunkhouse.

"So *that's* it!" exclaimed a big cowboy. "Trust Brad Dwyer to drop a loop on something of that sort. He did himself brown this time."

"I keep feeling I've seen him somewhere," grumbled a wizened old fellow with hard, bitter eyes back of a great hooked nose. "Seen him somewhere or heard a lot about somebody who looks like him."

"Reckon the last is more like it, Pete," said another. "If you'd seen him chances are you'd remember where and when. You don't see that kind and forget about it over soon. Them eyes! they go through you like a greased knife! And they give you the feelin' that you'd better not have anything inside you don't want looked over. There's a gent who, I calc'late, could give Tom Kane his come-uppance."

"Considerable of a chore," remarked a companion. "Say what you please about Kane, he sure ain't no pushover."

"What do you think about what Dwyer said—that there was no proof that Kane had anything to do with the Boss getting cashed in?" asked the first speaker.

"It sort of floored me," admitted old Pete. "Wouldn't have expected Dwyer to hand out that sort of a line, but damn it—the way he put it made it sound plumb reasonable. And the yarn about them damn goats we all figured to be sheep! Where in hell did he learn that, anyhow?"

"One guess," chuckled the big cowboy.

"One is enough," admitted Pete. "Brad was just repeating what that big feller handed out. Well, if *he* figured it that way, I'm of a mind to trail my twine along with him. But mind you he didn't say Kane wasn't guilty. Just said there was no real proof against Kane and that it isn't fair or sensible to jump before you know which way the pickle is going to squirt. Makes sense, all right. Guess we'd better sort of forget about cleaning out the Diamond T bunch."

"Guess we'd better," agreed the big hand. The others nodded.

Hatfield would have been decidedly pleased to know what fruit the seed he had carefully sown in Brad Dwyer's mind had born.

"Brad said that Hatfield feller was plumb riled against the Richardson bunch, whoever they are, for throwing lead at him," remarked Pete.

"Well," said the big fellow dryly, "if I was Richardson and found out that jigger was on the prod against me, I'd sure lay low while he was around. I got a notion that tangling with him is about like giving a grizzly bear the under-hold and first bite!"

Which, coming from a gent who could boast seven notches on the butt of his gun, packed considerable weight!

Hatfield sat and talked with Austin, Gaylord and the other oldsters till around midnight and then followed Brad Dwyer upstairs to the room assigned him. It was in the front of the house and overlooked the grove of widespread trees that shut the ranchhouse off from the trail. He did not light the lamp but drew a chair to the open window and sat gazing at the moonlight which silvered the trees. The night was very still. Only the drowsy murmur of conversation in the living room below blunted the sharp edge of the silence. The bunkhouse was dark. Evidently the hands had foregone their nightly poker game in deference to the dead.

Suddenly he leaned forward with an expression of interest. Somebody was walking under the trees in the yard below. The figure passed through a patch of moonlight and Hatfield recognized Mary Carter.

"Now what the devil's she doing prowling around outside at this time of night?" he wondered, his eyes fixed on the spot of shadow into which the girl had disappeared.

Quite a bit of time passed; then his keen ears caught a whisper of hoofs on the trail beyond the grove. The sound faded swiftly into the south. Hatfield sat watching, more interested than ever.

Finally the girl reappeared, walking slowly toward the ranchhouse, her head bowed. She passed beyond his range of vision, presumably to the back door of the house.

"Now what was that all about?" Hatfield asked himself. "Looks like she was going to meet somebody down on the trail. I sure heard somebody ride off just before she showed again. Maybe it was Wilson Brant come back for a word with her in private. Maybe she is interested in that four-eyed jigger. Guess he's the kind to catch a woman's eye, all right. But why should she meet him outside in the middle of the night? Looks like he'd just ride up to the house and ask for her. Well, as Brad Dwyer said, there isn't any accounting for what women will do."

11.

They buried Bill Carter under the whispering pines on the hillside back of the ranchhouse. A large crowd attended the funeral and curious glances were cast at the tall, black-haired man with the wide shoulders and the curiously colored eyes who stood beside Brad Dwyer as the body was lowered into the grave. Jed Kane was there, and Wilson Brant supporting Mary Carter. Afterward they rode away with the others. Hatfield and Dwyer walked to the ranchhouse.

"Miss Mary would like to talk to you a little later," the range boss remarked. "After we eat, she said."

Hatfield looked forward to the coming interview, but he was not exactly prepared for its surprising development.

Mary Carter entered the living room shortly after he and Dwyer had finished eating. She was pale and looked tired, which was to be expected, but Hatfield thought she was very charming in the simple black dress she wore. She came to the point with rangeland directness.

"Mr. Hatfield," she said, "Brad and I have been discussing you and I am following a suggestion he made. As you doubtless know, I'm not fitted to take over the operation of a big cattle ranch. And Brad doesn't feel that he is up to it, either. So I'm asking you to take the job of running the Cross C. What do you say?"

Hatfield considered swiftly. The proposition was not unattractive. He had a feeling that events in the section would focus on the Cross C, and it would give him an excuse for hanging around. He imitated the cow country's laconic acceptance of a proffered job, "Ma'am, I guess you've hired yourself a hand."

Mary Carter looked relieved and Brad Dwyer's face seemed to become one great grin.

"Now I feel a hell of a sight better," he declared. "I figured we were sure up against it."

It didn't take the Cross C hands long to discover that Jim Hatfield had forgotten more about the cow business than they knew or could ever hope to know.

"He sure is a whizzer," chuckled old Pete, the patriarch of the bunkhouse. "When he tells you to do something you know damn well it's the very best thing to do—no argument."

"I've a notion arguin' might turn out to be sort of unhealthy," big Val Bixby remarked. "Did you see him handle that outlaw bronc we brought in yesterday? I wouldn't have believed there was a man in Texas who could throw that horse. But he threw him, and didn't 'pear to over-exert himself doing it."

"Uh-huh, and after Hatfield held his head down and talked to him for a bit, that crazy-eyed killer got up and followed him into the corral peaceful as a manger-fed calf. Uh-huh, he's a man to ride the river with. Wonder if Miss Mary is going to fall for him? She sure looks soft-eyed at him when they're talking together. I'd take him over Wilson Brant any day. By the way, did you hear what Brant did? He showed up last night with that short-horn faced range boss of his and offered to lend him to Miss Mary to run the spread for her till she could get somebody else. Manuel, the cook, heard 'em talking and he said Brant seemed sort of put out when he learned she'd taken Hatfield on for the chore."

For three days, Hatfield rode the range with Brad Dwyer, familiarizing himself with the terrain. The evening of the third day found them down in the southwest corner of the spread.

"This is our best pasture," said Dwyer, "but we've lost more cows down here than anyplace else. It's a straight shoot across Tom Kane's holding to the Border. Over to the west is Wilson Brant's Rocking R, all good land."

Hatfield gazed at the dark and broken hills to the south. "Would be a considerable chore to run a herd fast through that jumbled mess," he observed.

"Uh-huh," admitted Dwyer, "but I reckon it could be done if you know the trails. Anyhow, they get through somehow."

"If they go across Kane's holdings," Hatfield commented. "What's it like farther south?"

"Good range beyond where the trail cuts over the rimrock to Bowman," Dwyer replied. "Long valleys with funny, low, dome-shaped hills jumping up unexpected. Covered with grass, though, and the sides not too steep for cows."

"Dome-shaped hills?" Hatfield repeated.

"Uh-huh, that's right. Look like big graves, almost.

They're always in the middle of the valleys. Steep slopes on either side all covered with shale and loose rocks. If it wasn't for them valleys, the range wouldn't be no good. Sort of cut up as it is."

Hatfield nodded, his eyes still fixed on the rugged slopes to the south.

"Anyone else ever try to buy that land that you ever heard of?" he asked suddenly.

"Why, no, not before Kane took over," Dwyer replied. "But I heard his brother tried to buy him out a few months back. Told Tom he'd pay him what he put into it if he'd just get out of the section before he started more trouble. Understand Tom told him to go to hell, that he wasn't going to be run out by anybody in any way."

"Jed Kane was trying to do his brother a favor, eh?" Hatfield remarked.

"That's the way folks felt about it," answered Dwyer. "Guess Tom felt the same way, 'cause I understand he cooled down and thanked Jed for his offer. But he refused to take him up on it. Said he hadn't done anything wrong in the section and wasn't going to slide out with his tail between his legs."

"Understandable enough," Hatfield commented.

"Uh-huh, but not over-sensible. Tom knows that plenty of folks figure he's Richardson, the owlhoot, and that something bad is likely to bust loose any time. And if it does, I mean it'll be bad. There are other folks who side with Kane. They'd side with anybody who's against the big owners."

"We can do without a range war in this section," Hatfield commented.

"You're darn right," agreed Dwyer. "Other folks are of the same way of thinking. I got a notion that's the real reason why Jed Kane tried to buy out Tom. He must have had a good reason for putting out money. It ain't like him. He's always been almighty tight with a dollar. If Jed puts out a peso, you can just about be sure he figures to get two back. But if real trouble busted loose, he'd have to side with one faction or the other. And there's no real telling who'd come out on top by the time the last hand was dealt. Well, reckon we might as well be heading back to the spread. What do you figure to do tomorrow?"

"I think you and the boys had better start combing those north pastures for that trail herd we've got an order for," Hatfield replied. "The buyer seems to be in a hurry for those steers. Offered a bit of a bonus if we get them to him before the ninth."

"We'll get 'em," declared Dwyer. "The boys are feeling chipper the way you've taken hold. They weren't feeling so good before. Aside from Miss Mary not knowing much about the business, you know how cowhands are. Mighty few of 'em hanker to work for a woman. The oldtimers figure it's bad luck and they usually ain't got much faith in a female running things. And if fellers feel they can't depend on the boss, they don't give the best that's in 'em. You going to work with us?"

"I think I'll do a little more riding tomorrow," Hatfield said. "But the chances are I'll be with you before the day is over, to see how things are going. Yes, you can figure on seeing me before sundown."

"You be careful how you go riding around alone," Dwyer warned. "It's a sort of open secret that the Richardson bunch are out to get you."

"Hope to be there at the getting," Hatfield replied cheerfully.

"Okay, but don't underestimate those skunks," said Dwyer. "They're bad. They've done proved that during the past six months. If the Boss had listened to advice, and had a couple of fellers with him when he rode out, he might still be with us 'stead of pushing up the daisies."

"I'll keep my eyes skun," Hatfield promised. "Let's go—almost sunset."

12.

Hatfield was busy with office work all the next morning. Since Goldy was in pasture for a few days, getting a much deserved rest, the tall Ranger saddled up a stout bay shortly after noon and rode steadily west until he was close to Wilson Brant's holding. Then he turned south. He rode warily, constantly scanning distant ridges, groves and thickets. No bird or animal escaped his attention.

He knew very well that he was marked for vengeance by a smart and utterly unscrupulous outfit. Despite the apparent calm, he was not deceived. Apart from the desire to revenge the wounding of several of their number, the outlaws were doubtless uneasy about how much he had seen during the attack on Bill Carter. They could not be sure just how good a look at them he had had. They might very well fear that he had seen enough to be able to recognize one or more of them. If so, the quicker he was eliminated the better it would be for their peace of mind. He did not think they would risk an attack on the open range, but he was taking no chances.

Hatfield rode south at a fairly fast pace and it was not too late in the afternoon when he approached the dark and broken hill country that was Tom Kane's northern range. The rocky, brush-covered hills interested the Lone Wolf. They reminded him of scenery he'd seen in other sections of the state. He reached the point where Brad Dwyer had told him the Cross C range ended, pulled up and rolled a cigarette. He smoked thoughtfully for several minutes studying the bleak slopes. Then he pinched out the butt and spoke to the bay.

"We're going to take a chance and amble down there, feller," he told the horse. "If we run into some of *Señor* Kane's goat-herders they may take a potshot at us, but I rather doubt it. More apt to ask a few questions first and we'll risk being able to provide the answers." He shook the reins loose and ten minutes later was following a narrow ravine that trended in a southerly direction between two long slopes. He noted with interest that the slopes were largely loose shale of a bluish shade. A little later he pulled up beside a spring that gushed from under a creek.

"Reckon you can stand a mouthful or two of that ground travelling rainstorm," he told the bay.

The horse apparently agreed, for when Hatfield slacked off on the split reins, he bent forward eagerly and thrust his muzzle into the sparkling water. Then he jerked it back with a disgusted snort and shook his head vigorously, throwing off a shower of glittering droplets.

"Now what the devil's the matter with you?" Hatfield wondered. He dismounted, scooped up a handful of the water and tasted it. He spat it out as quickly as had the bay. It was bitterly salty. He straightened up and eyed the bubbling spring.

"Now this *is* interesting," he mused aloud. "Blue kerogen shale and salt springs! Horse, we're going to travel a bit and see what else we can find! I'm beginning to get a notion that may explain some of the funny goings-on in this section. We're going to play a hunch, and if the hunch turns out to be a straight one, we may have gone a long way toward settlin' this mess. Let's go!"

A mile or so farther on, the ravine turned into another that ran in a more southwesterly direction. Down this narrow valley ran a swift and turbulent creek.

Hatfield paused to taste the water and found it to be fresh and sweet.

"Just as I expected," he told the bay as he allowed him to drink his fill.

The shale slopes had been replaced by tall, bluish cliffs between which the streams roared with a hollow, tearing sound. Another mile and Hatfield heard a low rumble somewhere ahead. The sound increased in volume as he rode and he knew it must come from a waterfall of considerable height. A little later he caught sight of it.

The creek plunged over a precipice of some thirty feet in height. The valley floor rose sharply here and the chunky horse had a hard scramble to make it up the broken ground farther on. The slope which was sudden and abrupt seemed to have no apparent reason for its existence.

"It wouldn't be here," Hatfield reasoned, "unless there had been a considerable subsidence of strata to the north a long time back. A wide section of ground does not sink without some subterranean reason. And the cliffs have been replaced by shaly slopes."

Beyond the waterfall the ground was broken, with the scatter of gigantic boulders and the evidence of fallen reef. Between these the horse picked his way cautiously. Hatfield studied the formations with ever-increasing interest.

He was a couple of miles beyond the waterfall now and so intent on the terrain over which he was riding that for the moment he had forgotten all else. Only the uncanny sixth sense that develops in men who ride often with danger saved him. At the sudden pricking of his horse's ears and its questioning snort, Hatfield glanced quickly ahead. A gleam flickered among the rocks. He slowed his mount sharply, at the same instant hurling his body downward behind the animal's neck.

As it was he felt the wind of the passing bullet. Then

the rocks ahead seemed alive with the mounted men who swarmed into view, yelling and shooting.

Hatfield's hand streaked downward. With a bitter curse he remembered that the light rig he was using to accommodate the bay's strength was not equipped with a saddle boot. His big Winchester rifle was at the ranchhouse.

Six-guns against rifles at that range! Suicide, nothing less! He whirled the bay and sent him charging back down the gorge. Bullets stormed all about him, flicking bits of stone into the air, kicking up puffs of dust, fanning his cheeks with their lethal breath. Hatfield risked a glance over his shoulder. The pursuers, nearly a dozen of them, were coming at full speed. That fleeting glance told him that they were masked.

"Not taking any chances on being recognized," he muttered. "Well, the way things are working out, they're not taking much of a chance." He bent low in the saddle and gave all his attention to getting the last ounce of speed out of his horse. If he could reach the steep and broken slope where the creek plunged over the cliff, he might make it to the bottom and hole up for he saw that he could not hope to outrun the pursuit. Were he forking Goldy, there would have been nothing to it. He could have gained distance and drawn out of the shooting range of mounted men. But he wasn't forking Goldy!

The bay was doing the best he could, but he was not the horse for fast work over broken ground. Had Hatfield been riding the great sorrel with his phenomenal speed and endurance, it would have been an exhilarating though dangerous game of tag instead of the grim race with death that it was. He bitterly cursed his preoccupation with the geological phenomena which had allowed him to ride into an ambush.

But the damage was done. All he could do was make the best of it. And as the bay stumbled and floundered over the rocks he grimly admitted that the best was not good enough. The pursuers were gaining. If they pulled up and took careful aim they'd down him in a hurry. And they were very likely to do so at any moment.

Ahead loomed the blue curve of the fall. The roar of it was in Hatfield's ears, dimming the crackle of the rifles and the excited yells of the pursuers. Maybe he could make it over the lip of the rise after all. Then he might have a chance. Once down the steep slope and onto the more open ground, the bay would do better. And just a little farther on were clumps of trees and thicket in which he might make a stand. His pursuers would have to close in on him then and his sixguns wouldn't be at such a disadvantage.

Suddenly it happened. Hatfield heard a sullen, thudding sound. The bay screamed shrilly, floundered, gave one convulsive leap and went down in a sprawling heap. By a miracle of agility, the Lone Wolf freed himself from the stirrups and jumped from the saddle as the bay hit the ground. He struck the ground with a thud and for an instant lay half-stunned. Stinging fragments of stone dashed into his face as a slug smacked a boulder only a few inches away from him. He staggered to his feet, reeling drunkenly, and glared about.

His horse was dead. Behind him sounded a thunder of hoofs, a roar of guns and a triumphant whooping.

But in their excitement the drygulchers were firing recklessly. None of the bullets found its mark. Hatfield glanced toward the slope. He could never hope to make it in time. He turned and ran to the bank of the stream. Quickly he made his decision. A few yards ahead was the curving blue lip of the fall. The foaming water rushed toward it at mill race speed and plunged over with a hollow roar.

Hatfield reached the bank and dived head first into the creek. The current gripped him, hurled him downstream with blinding swiftness. Beneath yawned the fall. He was over the curving lip, rushing downward, his head ringing from a grazing contact with a jutting rock. He struck the deep pool, gripped the jutting fangs of stone with both hands and, slowly and painfully, began crawling over the rocks.

The mighty weight of the hurtling tons of water flattened him against the bottom of the pool, pinning him down, retarding his movement. Pain flowed through his body from the jabbing of the sharp stones. His lungs were bursting. A red-hot band of steel encircled his throbbing temples. Before his eyes was a bloody mist. But still he struggled on, inch by tortuous inch, the last vestige of his strength swiftly ebbing away.

Whooping and yelling, the masked drygulchers reached the bank, jerking their foaming horses to a slithering halt. They stared downward, rifles ready for instant action.

But Hatfield's head never broke the surface below the fall. For hundreds of yards below the fall the creek ran straight as an arrow. Not even a rat could have passed unnoted by the watchful eyes of the killers, much less a swimming man. Finally with muttered curses they relaxed.

"He's a goner," said a tall man who apparently was the leader. "Well, that's as good a way as any. This creek runs into the Pecos, and the Pecos never gives up its dead."

"I'll sleep a damn sight better now," growled a hulking individual with thick, bowed shoulders. "I ain't felt right since that lanky cayote spotted us there on the river bank. Couldn't keep from thinkin' all the time that maybe he saw more than he talked about."

"Well, if he didn't talk about it before, he's not likely to now," replied the other. "You did a good chore of spotting him riding this way. What I'd like to know is why the hell *was* he riding down here? Maybe he did suspect something and was trying to find out for sure. Well, it doesn't matter any more. Let's go. I've got something important on hand tonight and it's getting late." He turned his horse and rode back up the ravine. The others trailed behind him.

13.

JIM HATFIELD HAD GAMBLED HIS LIFE on his knowledge of waterfalls, and he had won! Gasping, choking, shaking with exhaustion, he crawled out of the boiling catch basin of the fall and into the concave hollow between the cliff face and the rushing curtain of green water. Sufficient air for breathing purposes filtered through the spray and its opaque veil effectually hid him from view. He could hear nothing of what went on above, but he judged correctly the reactions of the drygulchers when he did not appear below the fall. He felt sure that even now they were confident his body was far downstream, hurtled by the swift current to the distant Pecos.

But he took no chances and remained crouched in his watery retreat. Despite the discomfort of his position, he was fascinated by the awesome beauty of the opaline curtain rushing downward but a few feet from his face. There was an ever-changing kaleidoscope of vivid tints and hues rolling, sparkling, glowing. The downward sweeping fall was as a constantly overturning dome of rainbowed color.

"Worth getting half drowned to see," he muttered, leaning against the damp rock, his strength gradually returning. "Well, those buzzards should be gone by now unless they've decided to make camp here, which I'd say isn't likely. Think I'll take a chance and get somewhere where it's warmer."

Drawing a deep breath he plunged through the thin

edge of the fall onto dry ground, shook the water from his eyes and glanced about.

There was no one in sight. He heard nothing save the rumble of the falling water. He climbed up the bank and sat down on a rock. Hot sunlight was pouring into the ravine and reflecting back from the cliffs. His clothes would soon dry. He tugged off his boots, and emptied them of water. Then he carefully fished soaked tobacco and papers from his pocket and spread them on the hot rock to dry. He had matches in a tightly corked bottle that had escaped breakage, and in ten minutes he had a cigarette rolled and going. Leaning back on the rock, he drew in lungfuls of the satisfying smoke. He glanced regretfully at his dead horse and shook his head.

"Just plain dumb luck I'm not like you," he told the departed animal. "Sometimes I think I need my head examined! Ride right into an ambush like that! Some owlhoot must have spotted me and circled round by way of a shortcut to get the rest of those hellions holed up till I came along. If I hadn't seen the glint of his gun barrel as he shifted it to line sights, he'd have got me with the first one! Oh, well, live and learn! That is, if you manage to stay alive. Which looked damned unlikely a little while ago."

He pinched out the cigarette and started on the long and arduous tramp back to the ranchhouse.

It was well past midnight when he limped through the last belt of thicket west of the Cross C *casa*. He reached the final straggle of growth and halted abruptly in the shadow. Directly ahead was the trail, less than half a dozen yards distant, and in the trail a tall man sat a motionless horse. Standing beside the animal, her hand on the saddle horn, was a girl that Hatfield identified as Mary Carter. As he stared in astonishment, the man leaned far over and the girl raised her arms to wind them around his neck, their lips meeting in a lingering kiss. Then she turned and walked slowly toward the ranchhouse, glancing over her shoulder from time to time. The man sat his horse until she vanished into the shadow, then rode swiftly southward. As he turned in the saddle, the bright moonlight fell full on his face. Jim Hatfield sat down on a convenient boulder, rolled a cigarette and remarked sententiously, "Well, I'll be damned!"

For some minutes he sat smoking thoughtfully. He felt that all of a sudden he had plenty to think about. Finally he rose to his feet and crossed the trail to the ranchhouse. As he walked through the grove he saw that there was a light in the living room. He stumbled wearily up the steps, shoved open the door and lurched into the room, closing it behind him. He heard a little gasping cry of fright, and halted, staring.

Mary Carter stood beside the center table, a book in her hand, her blue eyes wide and startled. She was clad only in a very becoming and very revealing nightgown.

"Jim!" she exclaimed. "What's happened to you? Your face is all scratched and there's a great lump on your forehead! And your clothes look like you've been soaking wet! What in the world—"

"Had a little bad luck," Hatfield mumbled as he sank into a chair. All of a sudden he was very, very tired. "I'm all right."

She ran to him, her eyes dark with concern, and passed cool, gentle fingers over the lump on his forehead.

"You don't look all right," she said. "You look like you're half dead! What—oh, good heavens!"

She had glanced down at her costume and her cheeks burned.

"Wait till I put a robe on!" she exclaimed. "Don't you dare move till I get back." She pattered up the stairs and returned in a moment wearing something that Hatfield thought went well with her blue eyes and golden hair.

"Don't say a word," she told him. "We can talk later. Come out to the kitchen and I'll make you some hot coffee and something to eat, if you feel you can eat."

"I could eat a live horse," he said, standing up and rocking a little on his feet.

"Lean on me," she said. "Don't worry, I'm strong."

Hatfield contented himself with an arm around her slender waist. They walked to the kitchen together. Mary immediately pushed him into a chair.

"No, you're not going to do a thing," she said. "I'll take care of everything. You just sit still and rest. You need it."

She shoved wood into the stove, on top of the coals that still glowed there and quickly had a good fire going. Soon coffee was steaming and meat frying in a skillet. In an amazingly short time she had an appetizing meal before him. She sat opposite him while he ate, her eyes never leaving his face.

"And now tell me about it," she said as she poured him a final cup of coffee.

Hatfield told her, in terse sentences. "You might have been killed!" she said when he had finished, and shuddered.

"Well, I wasn't, so guess there isn't anything to worry about," he replied cheerfully.

"And I would have felt I was to blame, for talking you into taking a job and staying here."

"Guess I'd have stayed anyhow," he answered laconically.

She regarded him steadily for a moment, her round, white, little chin cupped in her hand.

"Jim," she said, "just who and what are you?"

"What do you mean by that?" he parried.

"I mean," she said, "that you are no ordinary cowhand, and I don't think you have been one for a long time."

"Why?"

"Hold out your hands," she said. "I may not know

how to run a ranch, but I've been thrown in with cowboys all my life. I've noticed certain definite marks of their profession. You have no marks of rope or branding iron on your hands."

"Good eyes," he commented.

"And your manner of expressing yourself is not that of a cowhand," she added.

Hatfield studied her face a moment and arrived at a decision. He fumbled with a cunningly concealed secret pocket in his broad leather belt and laid something on the table between them. She stared at the familiar silver star set on a silver circle.

"A Texas Ranger!" she breathed.

"Correct!" he agreed.

"And why are you here?" she asked. "Are you looking for—for somebody?"

"Several somebodies, I'd say," he returned grimly. "I'm here to find out who's been raising all the hell in this section and to try and do something about it."

She was silent for a little while. Then, "You say you were down on Tom Kane's land when those men attacked you?"

"That's right."

"And you didn't see who they were?"

"They were masked."

Again she was silent. She drew a deep breath and her eyes met his squarely.

"Jim," she said, "do you believe Tom Kane killed my father?"

Hatfield smiled. "Well, after tonight I'm inclined to doubt it," he replied. "And I don't think you believe he did, judging from the way you kissed him goodnight."

Her eyes widened. "You—saw—"

"Yep," he replied. "I was over at the edge of the thicket. And I think I understand now why Kane, who doesn't 'pear to be the sort to duck a fight, turned his back on your dad when he braced him in town a while back."

"Yes, he told me about that," she said. "Funny how things happen, isn't it? I ran into Tom down on the trail not long after I came here to live with Dad. One of my reins had broken and my horse was running away. I didn't give it much thought because I can ride and I knew he'd run himself out in a little while; but Tom came riding along just then and stopped him. We got to talking and—well, it happened. And things were a mess."

"Still are," Hatfield said. "But I've a notion they'll straighten out after a while, so don't go worrying your pretty head about it too much."

She smiled tremulously as they stood up. "Somehow after tonight I don't think I will worry so much," she said. "You're a—a very comforting person."

Hatfield smiled down at her and cupped her chin in his hand. Her wide eyes looked up into his. He leaned over deliberately and kissed her on the mouth. She blushed prettily but her lips responded to his.

"That's one *he* won't get," Hatfield chuckled as they drew apart.

"Darn you!" she said, her eyes laughing. "You're the kind that breaks up a nice romance! You—you tomcat!"

"Tomcats have their uses," he replied airily. "And now, little lady, it's time you were in bed."

They ascended the stairs together. At her door, she paused.

"You'll be careful, won't you, Jim? I'd—I'd feel terrible if—anything happened to you!" She closed the door, very softly.

Hatfield slept late and awoke to a blazing hot morning. Aside from being a bit stiff and sore he felt little the worse for the preceding day's misadventure. He reached for his clothes and paused, staring.

They were right on the chair where he had left them,

but they had been neatly ironed, his water-stiffened boots oiled and polished.

"Well, that's what I call service," he chuckled as he donned the garments.

He found Mary in the living room when he descended the stairs. "I gave orders you weren't to be disturbed," she said. "I felt you needed your rest. Your clothes? Oh, I figured they needed some attention, too, so I slipped in and got them while you were still asleep."

"I'm sure much obliged," he said, "but that's the first time anybody ever entered my room without awakening me."

"A woman's step is light," she smiled, "and you were sleeping like a baby. Hope you don't mind." .

"The only thing I mind," he grumbled, "is that I didn't wake up while you were within arm's reach."

"Lost opportunity!" she giggled and danced out to the kitchen to supervise the preparation of his breakfast.

14.

BEFORE HATFIELD FINISHED EATING, the Cross C had a visitor. A horse pulled up in front of the ranchhouse and Mary went out to investigate. A moment later he heard her say,

"Why, hello, Wilson! How are you? Come right back to the kitchen. Jim's eating his breakfast. He was up late last night."

She appeared in the doorway with Wilson Brant. The Rocking R owner nodded cordially to Hatfield, then shook his head in puzzled fashion.

"Didn't expect to see you here," he remarked pleasantly. "I'd figured you were going to work for John Gaylord."

"Miss Mary sort of got the jump on John," Hatfield replied, his keen eyes fixed on Brant's shirt front.

Brant sat down and accepted a cup of coffee. "Got news," he said. "The Richardson bunch struck again last night. Grabbed off a herd over to the Tree L to the west of my place."

"How do you know it was the Richardson bunch?" Hatfield asked.

"Who else?" Brant countered with a shrug of his broad shoulders. "Job had all the earmarks of their work. Night hawk found with a knife stuck between his shoulder blades. Must have been struck down as he rode past a clump of brush, just like those two Cross C boys were done in when Carter's herd was run off. Bob Livesay and his hands trailed them to the Rio Grande but lost them there, of course. Almost impossible to track them once they get into Mexico, even if we could. The Mexicans side with the outlaws and protect them. Bill Carter was the only man who ever got a herd back from Mexico, so far as I've been able to ascertain. Guess that's what got Richardson so hot against him."

Hatfield nodded but did not comment further. Brant finished his coffee, chatted for a few minutes about range affairs and departed. The Lone Wolf gazed after him curiously as he rode off.

"Mary, did you ever know that fellow to pack a gun?" he asked.

"Why, no, I don't think so," she replied. "I understand he is very short-sighted and that a gun would be of no use to him."

"Well, I wonder whose shirt he's wearing today?" Hatfield remarked musingly.

"What do you mean by that, Jim?" she asked.

"I mean that I just can't understand how a fellow that never packs a gun should have the marks of double cartridge belts on his shirt," Hatfield replied. "Not very plain, hardly noticeable, in fact, but could be seen by somebody with good eyes. It's a hot day and on a hot day you're sure to sweat a bit under your cartridge belts, and sweat stains cloth. The stains are there, on Brant's shirt."

The girl stared at him open-eyed. "But—but why should he pretend that way?" she asked.

"That's your question," Hatfield rejoined. "Packs guns he can't see to shoot with, and wears glasses he doesn't need to see with. Quite a combination!"

"Glasses he doesn't need to see with! What makes you think so?"

"Well," Hatfield replied dryly, "a jigger who can read the label on a tequila bottle clean across the Rocking Chair barroom without 'em, sure doesn't need 'em." He related the incident of Chuck Taylor, Brant's range boss, and the bottle of tequila.

Mary looked bewildered. "I don't understand it," she said.

"Well," Hatfield admitted frankly, "I don't either."

Hatfield decided to ride up to the north pastures and give Dwyer and the boys a hand with the trail herd. He was still greatly interested in Tom Kane's land, but he didn't feel up to another ride through the south hills at the moment. The last one had been a trifle hectic even for the Lone Wolf. There was no doubt but that somebody was keeping pretty close tabs on his movements and he was not inclined to provide another opportunity where the odds were all against him. His next visit to Kane's Diamond K holdings, he decided, would be a more direct approach.

Also he was still quite a bit uncertain about Tom Kane. Abruptly a motive for Bill Carter's killing had appeared. With Carter alive, a marriage between Kane and Mary was just about out of the question. With Carter removed from the scene, no insurmountable obstacle remained. And the Cross C was a very valuable property. If Kane was as ruthless as a good many people seemed to think, he would not stop at murder to attain his objective. And Kane *had* been in town the night Carter was killed. Carrying the deduction a bit farther, Kane had doubtless spotted him and Doc Beard in the Rocking Chair. He might have deduced that Carter had been left alone in the office. Even the presence of Sam Whitlock would not have necessarily deterred him. Nevertheless, nothing had been proven against Kane and it wasn't likely that Whitlock would have suspected that the intended murder when and if he entered the office. Kane wouldn't have had much trouble throwing him off-guard for the moment he needed to strike him down.

The evidence was far from conclusive, but Kane, until proven otherwise, was a suspect, and as a Ranger, Hatfield couldn't afford to miss any bets.

It took three days to get the herd ready to roll. On the fourth morning, it headed for Bowman and the shipping pens. Brad Dwyer and the Cross C hands moved it along as quickly as possible for it was payday and the cowboys hankered for a bust in town.

"I'll meet you in town tonight," Hatfield told the range boss. "I've got some work to do in the office but I'll ride to town this afternoon."

Mary was anxious and worried when he set out. "Don't you think you should have some of the boys ride with you?" she suggested. "I can't help but feel you aren't safe alone."

"Oh, I don't think I've got anything to worry about on the open trail," he reassured her. "Besides I'll be forking Goldy this time and with a long gun under my leg, which will make a considerable difference. Going to wait up for me?"

"Darn it, I shouldn't, but I suppose I will," she admitted. "You're a bothersome and disturbing person. You've got me all mixed up."

"That's nice," he told her cheerfully. "Stay that way."

"Oh, go to the devil!" she replied. "But please be careful."

"Darned if I can see how a man can be careful going to the devil," he complained, "but I'll do the best I can. So long!"

Hatfield rode swiftly with a careful eye to his surroundings.

The ride proved uneventful. As he was nearing the old iron bridge that spanned the Pecos, where the trail turned over the rimrock, he saw a horseman approaching. A moment later he recognized Tom Kane. And as the Diamond T owner drew near, Hatfield made a surprising discovery. He pulled Goldy to a halt and sat with one leg hooked over the saddle horn.

Tom Kane also pulled up, half a dozen paces distant. He sat in silence for a moment, then,

"Name's Hatfield, isn't it?" he asked.

"So I've always been led to believe," Hatfield replied.

Kane looked puzzled at the answer. "Reckon you know who I am," he remarked.

"Reckon I do." Hatfield appeared noncommittal. Kane hesitated, apparently at a loss for words.

"Been hearing considerable about you," he said at length.

"And I've been hearing considerable about you, not much of it good," Hatfield told him.

Kane bristled a little. "Is that so!" he said. "And just what do you think of me?"

"I think," Hatfield said pleasantly, "that you're a bull-headed damn fool!"

Kane swelled and seemed about to explode, then suddenly he grinned, showing a line of white, even teeth.

"Feller," he chuckled, "I've got something of a notion you may be right; but why do you think so?"

"I consider that anybody who deliberately goes looking for trouble is short of gray matter," Hatfield replied.

"Trouble!" growled Kane. "Trouble's all I've ever known. I had trouble before I left here, had trouble while I was away, and I found trouble waiting for me when I came back."

"And never did a thing to prevent it," Hatfield retorted. "When Bill Carter jumped you about getting title to your land, instead of quietly showing him where he was wrong and you were right and straightening things out in a reasonable way, you climbed onto your high-horse and went swallerforking all over the lot. And I suppose you thought it was smart to let people think your Angora goats were just a breed of sheep that might get loose and ruin range."

"I didn't tell anybody they were sheep," Kane defended himself.

"No, but you evidently didn't take the trouble to tell anybody they weren't. No wonder folks are thinking you're most anything you shouldn't be."

Kane pushed his hat back, scratched his head and batted the rainshed down over his left eye. "Feller," he said truculently, "do *you* think I'm Jack Richardson the owlhoot?"

"No," Hatfield instantly returned. "You haven't got brains enough to be Richardson."

Kane shook his head and swore peevishly. "Feller," he growled, "you're the insultin'est hellion I ever met. I've pulled on men for less than what you've just said to me."

"Well, don't try it this time," Hatfield advised him. "That is unless you hanker to lose the use of that left hand of yours for the next two months."

Kane looked more surprised than afronted. "How the devil did you guess I'm left-handed?" he wondered.

"Well," Hatfield replied dryly, "I never knew a right-handed gent to pack his saddle boot on the right side.

When a man pulls a rifle from the boot, he pulls it across his chest."

"Darned if you ain't right," conceded Kane. "Now seeing as we got into this palaver somehow, I'm going to ask you one more question and then shut up. Do you believe I killed Bill Carter?"

"No, I don't, not now," Hatfield instantly replied. "In fact I know you didn't. I'd be willing to go into court and swear you didn't."

"Well, I didn't," Kane said, "but why are you so damn sure I didn't?"

"Because you're left-handed."

"Because I'm left-handed!" Kane responded in bewilderment. "What the hell has that got to do with it?"

"I examined the bodies of Carter and Sam Whitlock," Hatfield explained. "Whitlock was killed by a man who stood behind him. The blow caught him on the back of the head a bit right of center, which it couldn't have possibly done had the man who struck it been left-handed. And the handle of the knife driven through Bill Carter's heart was tilted a bit to the right. Had a left-handed man stabbed Carter, the handle would have been tilted to the left. It's impossible to strike a hard downward blow with a knife and leave the handle in a perfectly perpendicular position. It would be tilted one way or the other. Try it on a block of wood some time."

Kane threw out his hands resignedly. "Feller, you've got me plumb buffaloed," he said. "You ought to be a detective instead of a cowhand."

Hatfield let that pass. "I know you're not Jack Richardson, and I know you didn't kill Bill Carter," he said. "And I know something else."

"What's that?"

"That you're about as near a dead man as one can be and still keep walking around!"

15.

Tom Kane looked decidedly startled. "What the hell
—" he sputtered.

"I consider," Hatfield said, "that next to myself
you're the number one target for whoever is posing
as Jack Richardson. He's out to get you, and he will
get you if you don't watch your step."

"Hatfield," Kane said, "you've got me plumb scared."

"Nothing wrong in being scared," Hatfield replied.
"I was plenty scared myself a few days back." In terse
sentences he told the rancher of his experience in the
hills of his north range. Kane exploded.

"The snake-blooded buzzard!" he concluded. "Feller,
I'll tell you something. I've been shot at twice in the
past week. I've got a hunk of meat out of the top of my
right shoulder to show for the first one. The second
one turned my hat on my head. If I hadn't been riding
like a streak both times I've a notion I wouldn't be here
telling you about it."

"You're likely not to be so lucky next time," Hatfield
said. "You should never ride alone. Always have somebody with you. Two or three would be better. And
don't sit beside a lighted window at night. If you don't
give a damn about yourself," he added impressively,
"you might take some thought to the little lady up at
the Cross C."

Kane's jaw sagged. "Is there anything you don't
know?" he gulped.

"Plenty," Hatfield replied. "And now I'd like to ask
a little favor of you."

"Anything I can do," Kane instantly conceded. "Want somebody killed?"

"Not yet," Hatfield smiled. "I'd like to ride over your south range."

"Sure, why not?" Kane agreed. "Right now? It isn't very late. I was going up to my north pastures to see how my herders are making out with some critters we're ready to clip, but that can wait. Let's go!"

He turned his horse and they rode down the trail together. After passing the bridge they continued beneath the rimrock for about a mile and then veered to the left. The country was quite different from what it was farther north. The valleys were wider, the hills lower. It was good range. Soon they began passing clumps of cattle bearing the Diamond T brand.

"A nice holding; you should make out all right," Hatfield commented.

"Uh-huh, if folks would just let me alone and give me a chance," Kane grunted.

"Try giving them a chance and I've a notion they will," Hatfield advised.

"Sounds sort of twine-tangled, but I've a notion maybe it makes sense," Kane agreed. "Say, I'm glad I ran into you. You're the first jigger I've met in quite a while, outside of Wilson Brant, who acted real friendly-like."

"Wilson Brant's been friendly?"

"Uh-huh, he's been nice to me. He even got me and my brother Jed to talking again, after a fashion. Jed and me never did get along."

Hatfield nodded and gave his whole attention to the country over which they were riding. They were crossing a narrow valley which was hemmed in on either side by low hills. There were other hills visible, queer, dome-shaped hills starting up unexpectedly from the valley floor. Hatfield recalled Brad Dwyer's remark. They did look a little like big graves, short in proportion to their width. And they quickened the Ranger's interest.

"Any salt springs down here?" he asked suddenly.

"Why, yes," Kane replied. "Quite a few. Darn nuisances. And those damn bumps on the ground are nuisances, too. Clutter up the range. Fat cows won't climb the slopes, even though there's good grass on 'em. Never saw anything quite like 'em. No reason they should be there, so far as I can see."

"Sometimes folks can't see far enough, and then again some can," Hatfield smiled.

Kane looked puzzled, but the Lone Wolf did not see fit to amplify his cryptic remark.

They crossed a low ridge and descended into another valley with similar geological peculiarities. Hatfield turned in his saddle and gazed north. The general slope of the section was southerly, no doubt about that, although not at once apparent to the untrained eye. Kane's whole south range was, in fact, a great basin walled by the higher hills and cut by shallow ridges. The Lone Wolf was beginning to have a better understanding of happenings in the section.

"Somebody's smart," he mused, "damn smart, and with an unusual knowledge of geology and petrology, the science of rocks. Of course these signs are not conclusive—that has been proven time and again by wildcatters who sunk fortunes in dry holes, but they are very significant. A gent with no conscience doesn't mind gambling a little thing like murder against the chance of a fortune. Those hills to the north are kerogen shale and this basin was, a few million years ago, a vast lake or inland sea with the hills that now wall it in the banks. A perfect setting."

He tried to imagine the scene as it must have been before the coming of man—the rose-tinted waters of the sea glowing under a reddish sun, the banks clothed with a monstrous vegetation. On the beaches and sand spits huge, grotesque forms of life moved and ate and fought and died. The moonless nights quivered to a scream of agony as the greater dragon pinned the lesser among the slime. And always the towering and unbelievably luxuriant plant life grew and flowered and withered and died, and fell into the shallow waters, with sand and silt drifting over the decaying masses. Attacks of anaerobic bacteria removed the oxygen and the organic matter. Hydrogen and carbonic compounds predominated in the residues of the partial decay. The decomposition was finally halted through the complete covering of the material by later deposits and the accumulation of weight forced the mass lower and lower and the covering became thicker and thicker.

The hot lands heaved, mountains thrust up to the west and the north. The streams that flowed into the lakes were dammed and the evaporating waters grew shallower and shallower. The huge life forms perished and were replaced by others of a more active and more intelligent nature. But always the slow, unceasing chemistry of Nature worked wondrous changes in the vast deposits of vegetation to which had been added diatoms, algae, seaweeds and other forms of marine plant life. The precipitous banks of the sea lowered and rounded. Trees and grass found root on its bed setting the stage for the drama that was even now being enacted in the great basin with greed and hatred the motivating forces.

Hatfield came back from his dream of the past and turned to his companion.

"Kane," he said, "I was told that your brother tried to buy your holding. That right?"

"Uh-huh," Kane answered. "He came to me and said he'd give me what I paid for the holding if I'd just pull up stakes and get out before something really bad happened. I told him to go to hell. Then later he came back again and offered me considerable more than he did the first time. Said he was willing to take a loss just to prevent trouble for both of us that was sure to develop if I stayed on and kept feudin' with the big owners. He must have been worried bad, all right, for he was never one to part with a dollar if he didn't have to. He was always that way. His one aim in life is to get rich. He says if you got money you can do and get anything. Reckon he figured if I kept on going like I was, folks would turn on him, too, and he'd lose money as a result. I figured that must have been it, for Jed sure ain't easy to scare. He's a real quiet feller but he'll fight when necessary, and he's plumb pizen with a gun. I'm no slouch myself but he can make me look like a snail climbing a slick log. He killed a feller a long time back, a feller he caught cheating at cards. Stealing a pot he knew belonged to him was just about the worst thing anybody could do, from Jed's way of looking at it. Jigger was a tinhorn, though, and nobody thought much about it. Reckon most folks have plumb forgotten about it by now."

"And you refused to sell the second time?"

"That's right," Kane replied. "I've got my back up by then and I told him I wasn't going to be run out. He said I would end up getting killed, that the big owners were out to get me in one way or another and that they would. Maybe he was right. Things began to get tougher right after that. That's when the yarn that maybe I was Jack Richardson started going around, I believe. Reckon Jed had begun to hear things when he came to me the second time. He talked like he knew what he was talking about, all right. Reckon I am on considerable of a spot, with the sheriff looking at me cross-eyed on one side and the owlhoots looking for me on the other."

"Yes," Hatfield agreed, "you are. But if you'll listen to me maybe we can get you off."

"Feller," Kane replied fervently, "I'll listen to anything you say. I've a notion I'd lay down and roll over if you told me to. Got a notion you're that way with most folks. You're the talkingest hellion I ever met.

When you say something a feller just has to believe you and do what you say. And gosh!" he added with a grin, "you're up there living in the same house with my gal. I'm beginning to get worried."

"You don't need to," Hatfield smiled. "I've a notion she sort of likes *you*."

There was a moment's silence.

"Your brother has considerable education, hasn't he?" Hatfield asked.

"Uh-huh," Kane replied. "He went to college a couple of years, studying to be an engineer, like Dad wanted him to. He always did whatever Dad wanted. But Dad died about then and Jed saw he'd have to spend his own money to finish school, so he quit."

Hatfield received this interesting bit of information in silence, but the furrow deepened between his brows.

"Just a couple of more miles and we'll come to my *casa*," Kane remarked. "Why don't you come along and eat supper with me and meet the boys?"

"Wouldn't be a bad notion," Hatfield accepted. "Then I'll ride to town. Promised Brad Dwyer I'd meet him there tonight."

"Ain't but a couple of hours ride," Kane said, "and the sun ain't down yet. You'll have plenty of time."

The Diamond T hands were all young and, Hatfield quickly decided, a salty bunch. If real trouble developed between Tom Kane and his neighbors, there would be bloodshed aplenty.

"Quite a few small spreads to the east and west of mine," Kane observed as they enjoyed a smoke after eating. "Little fellers who got their land same as I did, most of 'em, though I reckon some are purty much nesters. They sort of stick with me. Ain't got much use for the big fellers."

Hatfield nodded thoughtfully. The situation was explosive.

A little later he got the rig on Goldy and headed for town.

"I'll be down to see you in a few days and we'll have another talk," he told Kane before leaving. "And don't forget what I told you about riding alone. Keep out of town as much as you can for a while."

"I'll do that," Kane promised. "As I said, I'm getting scared."

"I rather doubt that," Hatfield replied smilingly, "might be better if you were. But try and use a little judgment. It'll be better for everybody concerned. A steer isn't scared when he butts a barbed-wire fence, but all he gets out of it is scratches."

Kane chuckled and waved good-bye.

16.

HATFIELD HAD PLENTY TO THINK ABOUT as he rode through the lovely blue dusk that sifted down from the hilltops like a soft dust. Unexpected developments had forced him to drastically revise certain half-formed conclusions. Tom Kane, blundering, impulsive, hot-headed, was definitely not cast in the role of the shrewd and ruthless leader of the outlaw band that was terrorizing the section. He was just not the type.

"He couldn't get his hand in a barrel without making a noise," Hatfield told Goldy. "And he could never have written that threatening note to Bill Carter. Doubt if he would recognize the word 'retaliation' if he met it in the dictionary, that is if he ever saw the inside of a dictionary, which is doubtful."

Jed Kane, he felt, was due some earnest consideration. Doubtless a cold, avaricious man with a passion for money. And a man of considerable education. The question was, how much was Jed Kane governed by caution? How far would he overstep the law to attain his desires? Hatfield reasoned that he was the type that would carefully evaluate every step he took, would consider possible consequences as weighed against probable gain. But his greed might override his judgment.

But if Jed really appreciated the significance of the geological phenomena of Tom's holding, why had he delayed getting control of the land? Of course, he might have hesitated to offend his neighbors by taking up what was considered open range. Rather far-fetched, Hatfield was forced to admit, but not beyond the realm of possibility. Perhaps he had just been biding his time, confident that nobody would try to get title to land nominally claimed by Bill Carter and his influential associates. Carter had been an old man and couldn't last forever. The same could be said for others like Hilary Austin and John Gaylord. Jed, cautious by nature, might have figured it was to his advantage to hold off until the oldsters, in the natural course of events, were out of the way. And then Tom Kane came along and tangled the twine. Pure theory, of course, but up to the present, theory was about all he had to work on.

"And the fact that Jed studied engineering when he was in college sort of substantiates the supposition that he realized the potential value of that basin," he mused. "Not necessarily, though. There are many branches of engineering and all do not specialize in geology and petrology. Perhaps Jed didn't tumble to what that land might be worth until recently. Or maybe somebody who did realize its possible worth put him wise to it. That angle will bear a little consideration, too. Oh, hell! I'm just going around and around in circles and getting nowhere. Well, maybe

I'll eventually figure it out, if I live long enough, which last is a considerable question these days!"

Bowman was already booming when Hatfield arrived, shortly after dark. The hands from the various spreads had rolled into town for their payday bust. The bars were crowded. Gold pieces clinked on the mahogany and were echoed by the cheerful chink of bottle necks on glass rims. The poker tables were occupied, the roulette wheels and faro banks doing a roaring business. Boots thumped and high heels clicked on the dance floors. The short, spangled skirts of the girls whirled in a kaleidescopic shimmer. The vivid neckerchiefs of the cowhands provided an extra splash of color. The air was thick with tobacco smoke and tanged with the smell of spilled whiskey. Hatfield had an uneasy feeling that later it might well be tanged with the acrid taint of powder smoke and the raw and piercing reek of spilled blood.

"The boys are all in this time," said Brad Dwyer, whom he found at a table laying a foundation of steak and potatoes against future libations. "It's been a good season and a lot of the owners handed out bonuses. They got money in their pockets right now, but they won't have it come morning. Not that they'll give a damn. A cowhand figures money is to be spent. Some of 'em figure to make a killing at the games, of course, and here in the Rocking Chair they got their chance. Some of the places in town are a mite different. Dealers have sticky fingers. Not a good section for that sort of operation, though. Quick trigger-fingers hereabouts. Wonder if the Diamond T bunch are going to drop in? I see quite a few fellers from the little spreads over to the east and the west of the big holdings. Salty-looking bunch, ain't they? I'm beginning to believe you're right when you say that the open range is on its last legs. Those jiggers are here to stay, and they're beginning to outnumber the big outfits. Yep, I've a notion small spreads and fenced range are coming, all right, but I also got a notion there'll be trouble before things are straightened out."

"With law and order and general prosperity the final outcome," Hatfield said as he gave a perspiring waiter his order. "Be better for everybody in the end."

"Hope so," said Dwyer. "Have to admit I don't exactly like it. I'm a rather old feller and slow to change. Reckon you sort of get in a rut when you're used to certain things all your life."

"I've a notion," Hatfield smiled, "that you're a bit more progressive than you realize, and you'll be working for a boss who sees things the new way."

"You mean Miss Mary?"

Hatfield smiled and deftly turned the subject.

"See most of our boys are in here," he observed.

"Uh-huh, I told them they'd be better off here than in such joints as the Ace-Full and the Hogwaller farther down the street. But the feather-brained fools will be wandering out looking for girls after a while, and then hell knows where they'll end up."

"I gather that Wilson Brant and his bunch usually hang out in the Ace-Full," Hatfield remarked.

"That's right," replied Dwyer. "I understand that Brant owns a piece of that rum hole. And so does Jed Kane, I been told. Feller named Kearns is the big owner and he's a cold proposition. He usually keeps order but I think he sort of looks the other direction when a little smooth work is under way at the tables. Brant likes it there, though, for the games are big and the stakes are high. Brant is considerable of a gambler. Jed plays now and then and usually manages to win. I don't consider him much of a gambler. He picks the gents he plays against and is mostly just a little better than they are. Oh, I never heard of him being mixed up in cold-decking or anything like that, but a feller can play a square game and still sort of take advantage—say, he's cold sober and the other gents have a few snorts under their belts. Sometimes cards run funny and most anybody is likely to make a killing now and then, but I've noticed it's the feller who plays a consistently shrewd game who comes out on top of the heap at the finish. Jed Kane is that kind of a player. Different from his twin. Tom was always a plunger and usually came out the little end of the horn."

"Does he play now?" Hatfield asked.

"Hasn't touched a card, so far as anybody knows, since he came back," Dwyer replied. "Don't drink much any more, either. You know, I have a sort of idea that Tom learned a lesson or two the hard way when he was mavericking around. One thing's sure for certain, unless what some folks say is true and he really is Jack Richardson, he ain't been mixed up in any hell-raising since he came back here."

A little later John Gaylord, Hilary Austin and a few more owners drifted in and joined Hatfield and Dwyer. After eating they had a few drinks and talked over general range matters for quite a while. Finally, after the others had taken their departure, Dwyer stood up and searched the room with his eyes.

"Don't see hardly any of our boys here now," he remarked. "Drifted out somewhere. Wouldn't be surprised if we find most of 'em down to the Ace-Full. The big games down there lures 'em and the girls are a bit more free and easy. Bob Baker who owns this place don't approve of his dance-floor girls going out with the customers but they look at things different in places like the Ace-Full. What say, shall we walk down there for a look-see?"

Hatfield had no objection and they left the Rocking Chair and worked their way down the street toward the Ace-Full.

"Just as I figured," Dwyer remarked as they entered the Ace-Full, which was even larger and noisier than the Rocking Chair. "Just as I figured, here they are. Looks like there's a big game over in their corner the way the crowd's watching in that direction."

They strolled over to the table in question. From the tenseness of the players Hatfield judged that Dwyer was right. The game was for unusually high stakes. One of the players, he noted, was Chuck Taylor, Wilson Brant's range boss. He had plenty of chips in front of him. About his chair hovered a rather attractive dance-floor girl with an eye to a winner.

Taylor looked up, caught the Ranger's eye and glowered. For some unknown reason he appeared to have taken a decided dislike to Hatfield. Once or twice more, while Hatfield and Dwyer stood watching the play, he shot a black glance in the Lone Wolf's direction.

Two of the players cashed in their chips and quit the game. The dealer glanced around suggestively. "Any of you gents care to set in?" he asked. "Room for two more."

Chuck Taylor again caught Hatfield's eye. "What say, highpockets," he said in a jeering voice. "Like to set in a real game with real men?"

"Take the son-of-a-gun up on it," Dwyer growled to Hatfield. "If you need dinero, I got plenty."

Hatfield did not care to get mixed up in the game, but the Cross C hands grouped around looked at him eagerly. So he nodded and dropped into one of the vacant chairs. He quickly saw that Chuck Taylor was not a pleasant player. The Rocking R foreman growled and grumbled whenever he lost a pot, and crowed offensively when he won, to the irritation of the other players, who seemed to be decent sorts.

As sometimes happens when a player doesn't take much interest in the game, Hatfield won at the beginning and continued to win, much to the disgust of Taylor. One by one the other players dropped out until Hatfield and Taylor were facing each other across the green cloth.

"Well, what you say?" growled Taylor. "Want to take the limit off? Just two of us left."

"Suit yourself," Hatfield replied, with a glance at the waxen-faced dealer, who nodded.

For a while the play see-sawed back and forth with neither obtaining any appreciable advantage. Then suddenly the showdown came. The dealer flipped the pasteboards, Taylor glanced at his hand.

"I'm standing pat," he grunted surlily, trying to hide the exultation in his voice.

Hatfield picked up his cards, studied them, hesitated, separated two cards from the others and then seemed to change his mind.

"I'll take one," he said, dropping the middle card onto the table.

Taylor glanced up quickly. "Feller's holding two pair and trying to draw to make a full house," he reasoned. He peeped again at his own hand and bet heavily.

Hatfield hesitated, glanced at his own hand once more and raised. Taylor promptly raised him back. Hatfield studied him.

"Got a little flush, eh, Taylor?" he said. "Or maybe it's a straight. Then again maybe it's a full house. Well, I'm taking a chance. I'll hoist her twenty more."

Taylor shoved his whole stack forward. "It goes as it lays," he growled.

The quiet dealer counted the money. Hatfield had enough in his own pile to cover the big raise.

"I'm seeing you, Taylor," he said.

Taylor smirked and spread his cards on the table, face up. "Nothing but a little full house, ace-high!" he shrilled, and reached for the pot. Hatfield shoved the grasping hand aside.

"Just a minute," he drawled. "I didn't have two pairs like you figured, Taylor. I threw away a king, and darned if I didn't catch another one in place of it! But I didn't care, Taylor; you see what I held onto was just four little deuces!"

The Cross C punchers howled exultantly. Taylor glared at the flock of two-spots spread before his eyes.

He cursed viciously and his hate-filled eyes seemed to spit flame. Then he rose to his feet.

"Damn you,, that cleans me!" he growled.

Hatfield glanced at the money on the table. There was a good deal of it, but he wasn't particularly interested in taking it. He decided to have a little fun with Taylor to even up for his unsportsman-like behavior.

"Wait a minute, Taylor," he said. "I'll tell you what I'll do. The little lady who's been standing beside you looks sort of good to me. I'll just play you the whole pile on the table against her, one hand of showdown."

Taylor stared in astonishment. All that money against a dance-floor girl who would go with anyone for a twentieth part of it! Then he understood Hatfield's meaning and his face grew more furious than ever. He wanted the money, but he hesitated to take up the challenge, realizing the fool he'd look if he lost. The laughter of the thronging cowhands decided him.

"Damn you, deal!" he exploded.

Swiftly the dealer flipped the cards. Everybody held his breath. A dead silence blanketed the crowded room. Hatfield smilingly turned his hand face-up. Taylor glanced at his and gave a yell of delight.

"Beat you!" he crowed. "I got three sevens and you ain't even got a pair! I win the money and the girl, too."

"Right!" Hatfield smiled as he stood up. "I'm right back where I started. Congratulations!"

The dance-floor girl who had been staring fascinated at the Lone Wolf suddenly raised her voice. Her clear tones rang through the room as she swayed around the table and placed her hand on Hatfield's arm.

"Come on, cowboy, and buy me a drink!" she said. "I'd rather trail along with a good loser any time than with a bad winner!"

The Cross C hands let out another jubilant howl and roared with laughter that was joined by the rest of the crowd. Chuck Taylor gasped like a stranded fish. Then his face flamed scarlet.

"Damn you! No, you don't!" he bellowed and reached for the girl.

Hatfield shoved his arm aside. Taylor reached again, mouthing obscenities. Hatfield gripped his wrist and this time the Lone Wolf wasn't fooling. Taylor yelled as the big hand ground his wrist bones together. Mad with rage, he rushed, both fists flailing. Hatfield stepped aside and hit him squarely in the mouth. Taylor reeled back, caromed off a chair and crashed to the floor. He came to his feet like a cat, spitting blood, teeth and curses, a gun in his hand. Men ducked wildly to get out of line. The room rocked to the crash of a shot.

Chuck Taylor reeled back with a howl of pain, clutching at the blood which oozed between his fingers. His gun, the lock smashed by the Ranger's bullet, lay a dozen feet distant. Hatfield, his gun still wisping smoke, instinctively glanced around the room, ready for instant action. But there was no need for caution. Everywhere men stood rigid. An awed voice said, "Gents, did you see that draw!"

"See it, hell!" said another. "Nobody could see it! That shootin' iron just *happened* in his hand."

Hatfield holstered his gun and walked over to the cursing Taylor, who cringed away from him.

"Taylor," he said, "you're either drunk or plumb loco. Get out of here. And leave your gun at home till you learn to use it. You've no more business packing one than your boss has with his bad eyes."

"Bad eyes!" stormed Taylor. "Why, damn you, he'd—"

His voice suddenly died away, his face whitened visibly. Wilson Brant had walked in unobserved during the excitement and now was standing not three feet from Taylor and looking straight at him, his eyes glittering behind his glasses.

"Been getting into trouble again, eh, Chuck?" he said quietly. "Some time you'll do it once too often. *Get—out!*"

Taylor turned and slunk out without a word.

"I'm sorry, Hatfield," Brant said. "Chuck's all right, but when he has a few snorts under his belt he's terrapin-brained and gets a chip on his shoulder. I'll make sure he's headed home to bed."

With a friendly nod he walked out. Brad Dwyer's gaze followed his retreating form.

"You know," he remarked to the Ranger, "you know, I've a notion that maybe it's a good thing that jigger has got bad eyes and doesn't pack a gun. Strike's me he's a cold proposition."

"He is," Hatfield said soberly. He turned to the dance floor girl who had remained at his side during the ruckus. "Come on, lady," he said. "I'll buy you that drink."

17.

THEY HAD A DRINK TOGETHER, and a dance. Then Hatfield rejoined Dwyer at the bar. The range boss was still thinking of Wilson Brant and the effect he had on Chuck Taylor.

"One thing's sure for certain," he remarked. "Chuck's scared of Brant. He turned all colors when Brant called him down and he didn't argue a bit when Brant told him to get out."

"Maybe he's afraid of losing a good job," Hatfield suggested.

Dwyer shook his head. "Wasn't that kind of scaredness," he disagreed. "It was the kind a dog shows when he knows he's goin' to be whipped bad. If he'd had a tail, it would have been right between his legs. And Chuck Taylor never struck me as the sort that scares easy. Even after you shot his iron out of his hand and showed you could have downed him just as easy, he still had his bristles up. Brant's got him buffaloed somehow. Well, maybe he's got something on the horse-faced hellion. Wouldn't be surprised if Chuck's been mixed up in plenty he shouldn't ought to have been. He looks it."

"Could be," Hatfield admitted thoughtfully. "Well, don't you think we've had enough action for one night?"

"That's the way I feel," Dwyer admitted. "Let's see what the boys have to say."

Several of the older hands were also in favor of calling it a night, so they rode out of town in a body.

"Safer this way, too," said Dwyer. "Ain't nobody likely to tackle half a dozen of us. I get a sort of funny feeling along my backbone of late when I happen to be riding alone, especially at night."

Mary kept her promise and was waiting up for him when they arrived at the ranchhouse.

"Well! back so soon?" she said. "She must have been rather disappointing."

"Oh, she was all right," Hatfield replied, falling in with her mood. "The trouble is I didn't run into her in her nightgown."

"You dog! I suppose you'll never let me forget that."

"I'll sure never forget it," he declared emphatically. "And if it wasn't for my *amigo* Tom Kane—"

"Your *friend* Tom Kane!" she interrupted, her eyes wide. "Jim, what do you mean?"

"Oh, Tom and I had a long talk and a long ride and dinner together," he replied. "We got pretty friendly."

"Then you really don't believe he—"

"I don't believe anything about him except that he's a dumb shorthorn with good taste in women," Hatfield said. "He sure needs somebody to look after him. You'd better get on the job before long."

He repeated in full his conversation with Tom Kane. The girl listened intently. She drew a quivering sigh when he finished.

"Now I just know everything is going to be all right," she said.

"Hope so," Hatfield answered. "Anyhow I'm going to do the best I can to make it that way."

"Jim!" she exclaimed, "I could kiss you!"

"Well, why don't you?" he countered.

Laughing a little, blushing a little, she did, and as if she meant it.

"That's enough," she said, "you're too darn disturbing. Well, anyhow, tonight I can really sleep for the first time in days."

"Not very complimentary to me," he laughed. "Go to bed!"

It was past sun-up when the last of the Cross C punchers straggled in looking considerably the worse for wear but with their faces ashine with pleasant memories. There was not much work done that day.

"But you'd better get over your headaches in a hurry," Dwyer warned them. "You're liable to have plenty to do tomorrow."

Dwyer was no mean prophet. About mid-afternoon, a buckboard drove up to the ranchhouse. A plump, jolly-looking individual with keen eyes descended from the driver's seat. Dwyer let out a bellow of welcome and ushered him into the office where Hatfield was busy with some paper work.

"Boss, this is Tim James, a buyer Bill Carter did a lot of business with," he introduced the fat man. "Hang onto the gold fillin's in your teeth. Tim don't miss no bets. He'd skin a flea to get the tallow. He's the reason poor old Bill Carter died poor."

James winked at Hatfield and shook hands. His plump-looking hand was hard and muscular.

"I just dropped in for a bite to eat," he said. "After dealing with this outfit for ten years I'm just a chuck-line ridin' buyer in a borrowed buckboard. Poor old Bill wasn't so bad, but this sheep-nosed misfit was always right beside him to squeeze the price up another notch. With a new man in charge who looks sort of human, maybe I'll be able to get my watch out of the pawn shop when I get back to town."

With the preliminaries satisfactorily completed, James got down to business.

"John Gaylord is running down a herd for us tomorrow, but it isn't nearly what we need to fill a big reservation order that just came in," he told Hatfield. "I'd sure take it kind if you could get me a few hundred head together pronto, as many as you can."

Hatfield glanced at Dwyer, who nodded. "Okay," he told James. "Today is Tuesday. How about next Monday afternoon?"

"That'll be fine," said the buyer. "We'll pay a bit above current market prices for quick delivery. I'll be waiting at the pens with a check ready soon as the weighing is finished. Sure I'll stay for supper," he told Dwyer. "That's all I ever get out of this dad-blamed outfit, a free meal. And I'll be expecting a bill for that in the next mail. Now please try and get us something besides hides and bones this time. When our plant manager looked at the last bunch we shipped him, he jumped into the Missouri River. Would have drowned himself if the water hadn't been so damn thick he wouldn't sink. Don't give him another chance or he might do better. When I left they were hauling spring water to mix with the river so the steamboats could navigate."

After Dwyer had left to see about supper, James

confided in Hatfield. "It's because Jasper of the Tree L had his herd widelooped the other night that we're on the spot. We'd been counting on Jasper's cows. For Pete's sake, don't let that happen to yours."

"It won't," Hatfield promised grimly. After a look at him, James felt pretty sure it wouldn't.

After an early supper James shook hands all around and drove off whistling like a blackbird.

"Nice feller," observed Dwyer. "Never knew a nicer. And he's a deceiving sort. Looks fat and soft and easygoing, but he ain't. Hard as nails, quick as a cat and plumb deadly. He often packs a lot of dinero in that old buckboard, for owners who prefer hard money to paper. But nobody ever bothers him. A couple of real salty gents tried it a few years back. Held him up on the road and told him to hand over the money. He said he wouldn't do it."

"And what did they do?" Hatfield asked.

"They died," said Dwyer. "James was doing his talking with a six-gauge, sawed-off shotgun."

As they sat on the veranda and talked, Hatfield deftly steered the conversation around till Dwyer, without realizing just how he got on the subject, was discussing Jed Kane.

"Jed's a fine cattleman," he said. "Runs his place right up to the hilt. He knows the business from the ground up. First-class with a rope and one of the finest riders I ever saw. Seems to be one piece with his critter when he's in the saddle."

Hatfield nodded and looked thoughtful. Somewhere in his mind was the memory of the rider who led the band that drygulched Bill Carter. He too had seemed a part of the very animal he rode.

Plans were made for assembling the shipping herd James wanted. "I figure the west pastures will be best for getting a bunch together in a hurry," Dwyer said. "The west and to the north. The brakes over there are easy to comb and there's plenty of cows holing up there in this hot weather. Good water and grass and shade in the draws. We should be able to make it by the time we promised him."

"Okay," Hatfield agreed. "Get the chuck wagon stocked up and send the bunch up there this evening. They should be able to make it by nine o'clock and they'll be all ready to start combing as soon as it's light. They've had a good rest today and shouldn't mind a little night work."

"They won't," Dwyer predicted cheerfully, "especially if you tell 'em to do it. Okay, I'll mosey down to the bunkhouse and start 'em hustling. Shall I ride with them?"

"No," Hatfield decided. "You and I'll ride over early tomorrow morning. Tell the cook to have breakfast ready so we can get started by sun-up."

Hatfield and Dwyer rode away from the ranchhouse as dawn was flushing the eastern sky with rose and gold. They rode swiftly, almost due west, aiming to circle around and join the hands who were working the north range first, estimating what the lower brakes would comb as they rode. They were almost to the beginning of Wilson Brant's holding when Hatfield suddenly pulled up on a stretch where the grass was sparse and the ground soft.

"What's the matter?" Dwyer asked.

Hatfield was studying the ground at their feet. "A lot of cows passed this way, travelling fast," he said. "Look at all those hoof marks. Must have been a few hundred sifting sand to the south. Horses, too. Look at the iron marks."

"And here come some more horses," Dwyer exclaimed, shading his eyes and gazing to the north.

There were nearly two dozen of them, all mounted, and fogging it for fair. As the hard-riding band drew near, Hatfield recognized, perched on the foremost horse, old John Gaylord, a wizened figure of wrath.

"The damn, snake-blooded buzzards rustled my

shipping herd!" bawled old John as he jerked his horse to a foaming halt beside Hatfield and Dwyer. "Killed two of my boys, too! I'm going to trail them to the Diamond T ranchhouse and clean out that nest of side-winders once for all."

Looking at old John, Hatfield decided he meant it. And a glance at his grim-faced hands told that they were ready to back him up in anything he started. Hatfield did some fast thinking.

"Okay," he said. "Brad and I'll ride with you."

The band got under way again, old John cursing and fuming, his men grimly silent. They gave all their attention to riding, but Hatfield's eyes never left the hoof prints scoring the prairie and constantly trending south. The trail was broad and easy to follow.

It was different, however, as they neared the dark hills of Tom Kane's north range. Here the ground was hard and rocky and the passing herd had left little trace. Hatfield's vigilance increased. They were well past the grassland and into the northern vestibule of the hills when his voice rang out, decisive, impelling. They were passing over a softer stretch of ground at the moment.

"Hold it!" he shouted. "Hold it, I say!"

The posse jostled to a halt. Old John raved and swore. Hatfield interrupted his tirade.

"John," he said, "the herd didn't go this way."

"Didn't go this way!" bellowed Gaylord. "What the hell's the matter with your damn eyesight? Can't you see those tracks? You—"

"Shut up!" Hatfield blared at him. "Shut up and listen to me!"

Gaylord swelled as if about to burst, but this tall, level-eyed cowhand had apparently usurped the authority. Gaylord listened.

"Yes, there are the tracks," Hatfield said, his voice quiet again. "The tracks of about twenty head, no more. And the tracks of two horses. The main herd turned off to the north of here. They sent a few steers and a couple of riders on south to make a cold trail for any possible pursuit. They figured some dumb shorthorns would fall for it."

Gaylord stared at the ground. "Damn you, you're right!" he exploded. "Now what in hell—"

"Back the way we came," Hatfield ordered. "We'll try and pick up the trail where they turned. Not too fast, now, it won't be easy. Keep a little to the west of where we rode down, so the marks our own critters left won't confuse us."

Hatfield rode ahead and when they were out of the hills and back on the rangeland he dismounted and proceeded on foot, his eyes scanning the ground. Suddenly he uttered an exclamation of satisfaction, stooped and picked up a boulder.

"Here's where they turned," he said. "Look at this rock. The damp side was up, showing that it had recently been kicked from its bed. Now, let's see. Uh-huh, here's a stone with a fresh iron mark scored on its surface. They headed due west. Right ahead now till we hit the grass over there. We'll pick up the trail easy on the softer ground." He mounted and led the way, quickening the pace. Five minutes later he pointed to the path by which a large number of cattle and several horses had recently gone.

"But what the hell does it mean?" demanded the bewildered Gaylord. "We're way over on Wilson Brant's land now."

"Naturally," Hatfield told him. "The only practical way to get south to the Border. I never believed it possible to shove a big herd through those hills on Kane's holdings with any speed. I rode down that way once and saw it couldn't be done. If you fellows hadn't made up your minds it was Tom Kane and his bunch did the widelooping, you would have realized it. Gents shoving a herd to Mexico don't get themselves tangled up in slopes and draws where the cows have to crawl. See, the trail's turning south, and so far as I can see from here on it's a straight shoot to the Rio Grande over easy range to travel. Are there any ranchhouses close on the way down?"

Gaylord shook his head. "Nothing within two or three miles," he said. "Brant's *casa* sets considerable to the west of here and Hilary Austin's is even farther over. Hatfield, damn you! you're right! Speed up, boys, them owlhoots are likely to get a surprise."

"How much start have they got?" Hatfield asked as he increased the pace.

"About three hours, maybe a little more," was Gaylord's abrupt reply.

Hatfield nodded, his eyes on the far distances ahead. The rolling rangeland was like the frozen waves of a sea, spangled with sunshine, the grassheads glowing pale amethyst against the background of deeper green.

"What you think, Jim, have we got a chance?" Dwyer asked.

"All depends on how successful they figure their ruse was," Hatfield replied. "If they feel sure they fooled any possible pursuit, their over-confidence may prove their undoing. I understand they've pulled that one before and left posses wandering around in the hills and getting lost."

"Uh-huh, quite a few times," Dwyer said. "The only time they got their come-uppance was when Bill Carter took that shortcut he knew, way over east, and circled them right after they'd crossed the Rio Grande."

"Then it may work," Hatfield nodded. "If they feel safe they'll ease up on the cows. They wouldn't want to try the crossing in the dark, that's sure, not unless they felt they had to risk it. And once they're in the wild country to the south of here they'd figure they were safe from chance observance. Yes, it all depends. Shove ahead and keep a sharp lookout. If they happen to have somebody hanging back under cover who may be able to spot us before we spot them, we'll get a reception we won't enjoy. It's a salty bunch with plenty of savvy."

"You can say that a couple of times," grunted Dwyer. "About ten miles to the River, now, and lots of brush and groves in between."

"Made to order for raiders," Hatfield nodded. "We'll have to take a chance."

18.

THE COUNTRY GREW WILDER AND MORE RUGGED. Long, low ridges criss-crossed the range. The visibility was poor; they could never see more than a few hundred yards ahead. Hatfield's face darkened as he eyed the forbidding prospect.

"John," he said to Gaylord, "I don't like it. If there ever was a section made to order for a nice drygulching, this is it. If the bunch ahead of us are what you folks call the Jack Richardson gang, they've got plenty of wrinkles on their horns. I can't see them missing any bets. We may be riding right into a trap and the first notification of it will be when we're mowed down. Listen, I want two of your best men. Brad and I will take them with us and ride east along the base of that next ridge. I see it peters out not far over to the east. We'll ease around the tip of it and ride parallel to the main body, and a bit to the front. That way we should be able to spot anything off-color before you fellows barge into it. Take it easy up the ridge and give us time to

round the tip and get a few hundred yards ahead of
you. Understand?"

"Okay, if you say so," grunted Gaylord. "Bob, you
and Russ go along with him. Hope you're not making
any mistake, Hatfield. If you are, it will give those
wideloopers a chance to lengthen their lead."

"I'm not," Hatfield replied shortly. "I've been
through this sort of thing before."

"Uh-huh, I'm beginning to have a notion you have,"
Gaylord returned, giving him a peculiar look. "Be seeing you."

Hatfield and his three companions turned sharply to
the east and rode at a fast pace. The main body slowed
down and breasted the ridge with their horses walking.

The four scouts rounded the tip of the ridge and rode
south. Ahead was another, lower ridge that extended
westward just a little past the eastern tip of the big
rise. They veered a bit and rode up the sag a hundred
yards or so from where it petered out.

"Plenty of cover here," Hatfield remarked, "and
from up top we should get a look at what's ahead.
Wouldn't be surprised if we can spot the River from
up there. Can't be far off now."

They rode swiftly up the slope and slowed down as
they reached its crest, threading their way through
thick and tall chaparral. In the final straggle of brush
to the south Hatfield called a halt. He pointed ahead.
There lay the silver coil of the Rio Grande, shimmer-
ing in the sunshine, its surface broken by a multitude
of black dots.

"There go the cows," Hatfield said quietly. He
shaded his eyes and gazed steadily at the moving
shapes.

"I see only six riders shoving them across," he announced. "And we've been trailing at least a dozen."
He turned and searched the sparse growth that clothed
the long southern slope of the big ridge to the west,
up the north side of which Gaylord and his men were

walking their horses. His eyes grew anxious as he estimated the time till the posse would reach the crest and
stand out hard and clear against the sky. He was confident now that an ambush was set on the slope. Unless
he discovered the concealed drygulchers before Gaylord and his hands reached the crest, they would be
riding into almost certain death.

Suddenly his keen eyes caught a shifting sparkle in
the growth. "Got 'em!" he exclaimed exultantly. "In
that clump of mesquite a hundred yards down from
the crest!"

"Right!" said Dwyer. "That was sun glinting on a
gun barrel."

Hatfield drew his Winchester from the boot. "Six
hundred yards and a little more," he estimated the distance. "Long shooting but we ought to be able to drop
the slugs close enough to rout them out. Let 'em have
it!"

The four rifles blazed as one. A moment later the
mesquite clump was violently agitated. Hatfield continued to fire as fast as he could work the ejector lever.

From the growth six horsemen bulged like pips
squeezed from an orange, and went careening down
the slope. Hatfield's eyes glinted along the sights of his
rifle. The long gun bucked against his shoulder.

One of the horsemen threw up his hands and pitched
from the saddle. Hatfield shifted the rifle muzzle a
trifle and fired again. A second man slumped forward
but kept his seat, reeling and wavering. Dwyer and
the others fired and a third owlhoot yelled. Then the
others were practically out of range and racing their
horses for the distant river.

On the crest of the slope a group of horsemen ma-
terialized as if drawn up by invisible wires.

"After the sidewinders!" Hatfield shouted. "Here
come the boys!"

But the way down the sag was rough and clogged
with brush. The fugitives drew away and were nearing

the river when Hatfield and his companions reached the level ground. They raced forward, old John Gaylord and the Lazy G outfit pounding after them.

At the river was intense activity. The horsemen abandoned the swimming cattle, sent their broncs plunging through the shallow water and streaked south. The wounded man also sent his horse into the river but the other two veered to the east and headed for a dark canyon mouth a mile or so distant. The foremost was a big, heavy-set man who rode with a peculiar heaving of his shoulders.

"That's the sidewinder who brought up the rear the evening Bill Carter was drygulched," Hatfield muttered as he urged Goldy to greater speed.

The great sorrel swiftly drew away from the posse's laboring horses. He was several hundred yards to the front when he reached the river bank. Hatfield veered him to the left and sent him charging for the canyon mouth into which the two outlaws were just disappearing. Yelling and cursing, Dwyer and his companions followed but steadily fell behind the flying sorrel.

Hatfield reached the canyon mouth but a few minutes behind the fleeing owlhoots. The walls were high and almost perpendicular. To all appearances there was no place where the fugitives could turn off. He was confident that Goldy's great speed and endurance would enable him to overtake them before they reached the far end of the canyon, wherever that was.

"If I can just corral that big hellion I've a notion I'll get to the bottom of this business " he told the sorrel. "Sift sand, feller, we'll catch 'em!"

He did, sooner than he expected. Goldy careened around a bend and not twenty yards distant were the two outlaws, both masked. They were sitting their motionless horses, guns in hand. Hatfield hurled himself sideways in the saddle.

. The quick move saved his life but it did not save him the stunning impact of a bullet that burned his temple. He jerked his guns and was shooting with both hands as he fell. Through a haze of red flashes he saw one man spin from his saddle, but the other, the big man, whirled his mount and fled up the gloomy gorge into which the sun had not yet penetrated.

Hatfield did not altogether lose consciousness, but the terrific blow of the grazing slug paralyzed his body for a few minutes and destroyed his coordination. When he was able to stagger to his feet, there was no sign or sound of the fugitive. He tried to mount Goldy but for another minute or so he couldn't make it. By the time he got into the saddle, Brad Dwyer and his companions came racing up.

"You all right, Jim?" the range boss called anxiously.

"Sure, except for an aching head that I think needs to be examined," the Ranger growled, rubbing his bruised temple.

"Let me look!" Dwyer exclaimed.

"You'd have to saw it open to find the trouble," Hatfield replied. "I was outsmarted, that's all. I barged right into this dark hole like a bull full of loco weed and they were waiting for me. Damn near blowed me from under my hat. The one I wanted got away, but I think I did for the other one. Let's take a look and see for sure."

He rode forward and dismounted beside the figure sprawled on the ground and jerked off the handkerchief that masked his lower features.

"Dead, all right," he said a moment later. "Ever see him before?"

There was a general shaking of heads. "Looks to be like an Apache breed," said Dwyer. "What do you think?"

"Sort of," Hatfield admitted as he methodically emptied the dead man's pockets discovering nothing of significance except a surprising large sum of money.

"Nothing to tie him up with anybody," he observed.

"We'll pack him to town. Maybe somebody there will recognize him. We'll get that other one back on the slope, too. Bring his horse over here. Skillet of snakes brand—Mexican burn. Doesn't mean anything. Load the body on the horse and we'll see how Gaylord and the others made out with the cows."

When they reached the river bank they found the exhausted herd pretty well rounded up on the north bank.

"And if it hadn't been for you, son, I'd have lost 'em," said old John, "to say nothing of getting my hide punctured. I won't forget it. If you ever want a favor from John Gaylord, don't hesitate to ask. Even if it's shooting somebody or burning down a church."

The body of the outlaw slain on the slope had been brought down. He was a hard-looking specimen with glazing black eyes and a cruel gash of a mouth splitting his lean face. Several of the Lazy G hands were of the opinion that they had seen him in town but were vague as to just where or when.

"One thing's sure for certain," Hatfield observed, "some of the bunch are well known in the section and would be recognized."

"How do you figure that?" asked Gaylord.

"Because," Hatfield explained, "they go masked. A real brush-popping outlaw outfit wouldn't take the trouble to do that. They've always got so much on them that when they pull a chore they don't give a damn whether they're seen or not. One more count against them doesn't mean anything. But somebody who lives here can't afford to be recognized. There are local residents with that bunch, I'll bet my last peso."

"That's what quite a few of us have been saying all along," Gaylord remarked significantly.

"And you've been saying wrong!" Hatfield snapped at him. "We've had about enough of that kind of loose talk with nothing to back it up. Gaylord, you're an in-

fluential and respected citizen of this section. You
should abide by the American principles of justice and
fair play and set an example for others. You said a
little while ago that if I ever wanted a favor from you,
not to hesitate to ask. Well, I'm asking one right now—
keep your mouth shut till you know what you're talking about!"

Old John looked dazed. His cowhands looked dumb-
founded. Nobody had ever dared talk to their irascible
boss that way. Hatfield's bleak glance swept over them
and they looked uncomfortable. Old John batted his
hat down over one eye and glared, his mouth tight.
Then abruptly he grinned.

"Hatfield," he said, "that favor's granted." He turned
on his men. "Hear what I said?" he barked. "You keep
a tight latigo on your damn jaws, too. All right, I
reckon those cows have rested enough. Head 'em for
town. We'll have to take it slow but I reckon we can
run 'em in by dark. Imagine Tim James is pawing sod
for fair about now. I promised him I'd have the herd
at the pens today. Much obliged, Hatfield, for making
it possible for me to keep my word. Let's go!"

It was after dark when they finally reached Bowman and turned over the herd to the greatly relieved
buyer. After the tallying and weighing were completed,
the outfit headed for the Rocking Chair and something
to eat.

"Everything's on me," Gaylord told Hatfield and
Dwyer. "I'm deep in debt to you boys. Hatfield, you
ought to be in the sheriff's office. I'm going to make it
my business to suggest to the commissioners that you
be made a deputy and stationed here. You've got the
makings of a fine law enforcement officer. It's a wonder to me you haven't got into that line before now."

The Lone Wolf smiled and deftly changed the subject.

While they were eating, Bob Baker, the Rocking
Chair owner, strolled over to their table.

"Howdy, fellers," he greeted. "Everything okay? Tom Kane and his boys were in this morning. They asked about you, Hatfield."

"That's nice of them," Hatfield replied. He slanted a glance at old John who turned red.

"You don't have to rub it in!" he growled after Baker left. "When you told me this morning I was wrong about Tom Kane, I figured I must be. But with Tom out of the running, what I'd like to know is who the hell is responsible for what's been going on in this section?"

Tim James the buyer, came bustling in and dropped into a chair, puffing and blowing. "John," he said to Gaylord, "can you get together some more cows? I've been doing a bit of telegraphing and the plant is yelling for more stuff in a hurry. Seems that big meat order I told you about is doubled. The government does things like that, you know. Hatfield has promised to have me a herd next Monday, but it won't be near enough. If you can double what we figured, Hatfield, I'd appreciate it. And John, what about Wilson Brant and some of the other boys? Think they can rustle some stuff?"

Gaylord looked thoughtful. "Tell you what, Tim," he said, "I'll get in touch with Brant and the Livesay brothers over to the west of my place and Whitcomb to the east. If they're agreeable, and you are too, Hatfield, we'll stage a little round-up. Nearly time for the regular fall round-up anyhow. Everybody's stuff is scattered over the various spreads at this time of the year and it'll be easier to round up everything at once and cut out. That'll be better than combing individual brands and turning everything else back—which is just a waste of time and effort. What say, Hatfield?"

"Don't see any reason why not," Hatfield replied. "Should think you wouldn't have any trouble lining up the others. We'll all come out ahead in the long run."

"That's the way I see it," James put in. "I want to hand this business to the fellers I've always dealt with.

The price is upped a bit because it's an emergency but I'd rather see you reap the benefit than folks I haven't had much to do with."

"We'll do it," Gaylord decided. "I'm heading back to my place soon as I finish eating and I'll start word to the other boys without delay. Thanks, Tim. I hope we don't get skinned this time per usual."

"I'm taking an awful chance," said James. "I'm taking an awful chance!"

Nobody who viewed the two corpses was able to recognize them. Several bartenders felt that they had served the leanfaced one at one time or another. But with so many strange riders coming and going all the time, that was not unusual.

The slain wideloopers were buried the next day in Bowman's "Boot Hill" cemetery. Doc Beard, the coroner, refused to hold an inquest.

"What for?" the testy old man demanded. "They're dead, ain't they?—and everybody knows who killed 'em and why. Take 'em out and plant 'em. I'm busy."

19.

HATFIELD AND DWYER did not remain in town for the funeral. The next day found them busy on the Cross C's northern and western pastures. It was little past sun-up when they left the ranchhouse but when they arrived at the north pasture, the general holding spot, John Gaylord was already there with his hands and his chuck wagon. Wilson Brant arrived shortly afterward.

Chuck Taylor glowered at Hatfield and did not speak.
Brant greeted him cordially.

Before noon all the outfits were on the ground. At
Gaylord's insistence, instantly backed by Wilson
Brant, Hatfield was chosen round-up boss and put in
charge of operations. His authority was absolute, for
it is an ironbound, rangeland custom that not even
an owner can question an order given by the duly ap-
pointed round-up boss.

Not that anybody wanted to. The assembled owners
quickly agreed that a better choice could not have been
made.

"He's one of these gents who's got a natural feel for
the cow business," saturnine old Caleb Livesay observed to Gaylord. "He knows just what's to be done
while other folks are trying to figure a way. A fine
young feller. And do you know, John, I got a feeling
I've seen him somewhere, or heard something about a
feller that looks like him."

"Could be," admitted Gaylord. "Brad Dwyer tells
me he was range boss for the XT. That's a whopping
big outfit, Caleb."

"One of the biggest in Texas," agreed Livesay, "but
I got a notion whatever I heard about him didn't have
anything to do with the cattle business. For the life of
me I can't get it straightened out in my mind. Ole Pete
of the Cross C feels the same way about it."

Hatfield's first chore was to select assistants who
would be in command of groups of cowboys that were
to scour the range in search of vagrant cows. He did
so without favor, picking the men he figured were best
fitted for the job. Among these were Chuck Taylor who
had the reputation of being an excellent cowhand no
matter what else he might be. If Taylor was surprised
at being singled out, he accepted the assignment with
a grunt that showed no emotion.

"I want all those brakes and coulees carefully
combed," Hatfield ordered. "I don't want any maver-

ıcks left hiding in the brush. Mavericks are a sign of bad combing. Any strays you run into, shove toward their home range. It's neighborly to throw over whatever you run into and it doesn't take much time. And we might as well brand anything that needs it while we're at it. Not much trouble and it'll save doing the same work again at the Fall round-up."

After giving his instructions to the riders, Hatfield went to confer with Gaylord and the other owners.

"I'd suggest we cut the individual brands into herds but keep them all here at the holding spot," he said. "That way we'll run the whole lot of them to town together, with all hands in attendance. These herds will represent a lot of dinero and if any gents with loose notions happen to be keeping tabs on us, they're not likely to try to make a raid on half a dozen outfits trailing together. However, I wouldn't put it past them to swoop down on a single herd even if it is carefully guarded. Plenty of good chances between here and town and they're salty enough without us giving them a break."

"After what happened to me, the other night, I'm expecting anything," declared John Gaylord. "We sure can't afford to miss any bets." The others nodded emphatic agreement.

The troop of cowboys rode off over the range, spreading out and dividing into small parties, scattered at distances varying with the topography of the country. Each man had to hunt out all the cattle on the ground over which he rode.

The cattle were gathered up by ones and twos and driven to the holding spot on the Circle C north pasture. As soon as these "circle riders," had driven their quarries onto the holding spot they surrounded the captured cows and held them in close herd.

Next the riders changed horses and rode into the herd to cut out the various brands. To complete this job bold and skillful horsemanship was necessary inasmuch as the greater part of the herd retaliated with splaying hoofs and needle-pointed horns.

As the cows were separated from the main herd they were driven before the tally man who called the brands, kept count and directed the distribution to the various subsidiary holding spots assigned to individual owners, where they were again held in close herd until ready for the trail.

It was on the afternoon of the third day that Hatfield made a momentous discovery. Drifting from one section to another to keep a close watch on the work, he came to a bit of range that was being combed by Chuck Taylor and the men directly under his command. It was a rough terrain and a favorite hole-up for tough, old longhorns who preferred to live in solitude. Rarely were more than two found hanging out together, but two were enough to keep any skilled cowhand busy.

Taylor flushed a big fellow from a gulch. Away went the angry cow at breakneck speed with Taylor in close pursuit. Hatfield started to ride to his assistance and then suddenly jerked Goldy to a halt and sat staring after Taylor.

"Well, I'll be damned!" he remarked aloud.

Chuck Taylor's posture while riding at full speed was peculiar. He leaned far forward and made a heaving movement with his big shoulders with each forward stride of his horse, as if he were lifting the animal instead of being carried by it.

"Well, if this don't take the shingles off the barn!" Hatfield told the sorrel. "You run all over hell looking for something and all the time it's right before your eyes. There goes the big hellion who was bringing up the rear when Bill Carter was drygulched down on the Pecos. And that fancy-riding gent leading the pack wasn't Jed Kane. *That* was Wilson Brant! Wilson Brant without his phony glasses and with a couple of guns strapped around his waist. Carter must have got a look at him when they jumped him on the trail. That's why Brant came snooping into Doc Beard's office right after I brought Carter in. And that's why he slipped back later and killed Whitlock and stuck a knife between Carter's ribs. Had to make sure he wouldn't get his senses back and talk. The snake-blooded devil!"

Things began to fall into place for Hatfield. Wilson Brant had got the Kane brothers together so Jed could try to persuade Tom to sell his holdings. It was not insignificant that Brant's eyesight was not nearly as bad as he pretended it was and that he did pack guns at times. And he was always around when something busted loose, or he showed up immediately afterward. It would have been easy for Brant to fool poor Sam Whitlock who had no reason to be suspicious of him. He could have slipped out of the Ace-Full without attracting attention to himself, perhaps by way of a back door, seeing as he had an interest in the place, committed the double murder and been back in a few minutes. Had an alibi all set up if he happened to need one. And Brant was undoubtedly an educated man, his mode of speech evidenced that. Brant would have been capable of writing the note found in Bill Carter's pocket. Maybe it was Brant who had started the talk about Tom Kane whose holding he coveted. It was Brant, Hatfield reasoned, who first realized the value of Tom Kane's holdings. Then he played on Jed Kane's greed and got him to go along with him in the scheme to acquire the land. Hatfield recalled that people insisted they'd seen Tom Kane in the vicinity right before or right after something had been pulled. They didn't. They saw Jed Kane who so much resembled his twin that at a distance nobody could tell the difference—Jed Kane, skillfully planted by Brant.

The Ranger smiled suddenly. It was a mighty nice deduction, but, he knew very well, not worth a damn in a court of law. A skillful lawyer could pick it to pieces in no time.

"If I could just afford to risk it, I'd have Captain Bill backtrack a little on Brant's trail and see if he couldn't dig up something on him," the Ranger mused. "But I can't take the chance. That would take time, and leaving him running around loose is very likely to mean that there'll be more killings."

Something else persisted in Hatfield's mind. Maybe the slaying of Bill Carter had several causes. It was not only that Carter had posed a threat to the outlaw faction. Brant was undoubtedly interested in Mary Carter, with an eye to the very valuable Cross C ranch. He had not known of course that the reason the girl was not more receptive to his advances was that she'd fallen hard for Tom Kane. Doubtless Brant's cold, calculating mind had reasoned that with her father dead she would welcome his proffered assistance in running the ranch and from then on it would be easy going for him.

"The little jigger with the arrows often manages to gum up the works," Hatfield chuckled. "Well, if I'm to play understudy to Cupid, I only hope I don't make hash of it. Guess the only thing it to lay a trap for that hellion and hope he'll walk into it. If he doesn't catch on to me, I've a notion I'll hook him. I figure he'll go to great lengths to prevent Tom Kane from learning the value of his holding. If I can just make the thing look harmless enough, I believe it'll work. Anger and greed don't make for clear thinking and I'll have both working for me. I'll have a little talk with Tom Kane as soon as this chore is over. Don't think I'll have much trouble getting him to go along with me. If he balks, I'll sic Mary on him! She'll bring him around in a hurry."

The round-up proceeded without incident. Gaylord and the other owners were highly pleased with the way Hatfield handled the chore.

"You'll be round-up boss for the whole section when

we start the big one this fall," old John declared. The others echoed his remarks.

Sunday afternoon Mary Carter rode in to give the round-up a once-over. Hatfield thought she appeared very happy and very pleased about something.

"Well, what is it?" he asked when they were alone. "You look like a tabby-cat that's just lapped up a saucer of cream."

"Tom was up to the house last night," she confessed. "The cook and the wranglers had gone to town and I thought it was safe to let him come in."

"Fine!" Hatfield applauded. "Did he catch you in your nightgown?"

"Uh-huh!"

"Nice going," Hatfield commented. "What you blushing for?"

"The sun's hot," she parried.

"Been behind the clouds all day. Looks like it might rain."

"But, Jim, I'm scared," she said. "He finally admitted that you told him he's in grave danger. He didn't mean to tell me but he let a word slip and I got it out of him."

"Not surprised," Hatfield answered. "Under certain circumstances a man will tell anything—to a woman. But don't go worrying your pretty head about it. I've a notion everything is going to work out and soon. Hope I'll have time to stay for the wedding."

"If you don't, I'll never speak to you again," she told him vigorously. She was smiling when she rode back to the ranchhouse and appeared reassured.

But Hatfield was not so optimistic as he sounded. He was genuinely worried about Tom Kane. And he did not underestimate the man pitted against him. Wilson Brant might prove a little too shrewd to fall for the ruse Hatfield contemplated. Maybe he'd out-maneuver him. That he was deadly, resourceful and possessed of cold courage he had amply proven. Hatfield wondered if he really was the famous outlaw Jack Richardson. Didn't matter much whether he was or wasn't. He was plenty bad in his own right.

20.

EARLY MONDAY MORNING the big herd took the trail. The route chosen was around the rugged hill country of Tom Kane's northern range, across the holdings of Wilson Brant and Hilary Austin to reach Bowman from the west. Hatfield figured they should make it to town by dark with one stop at noon for lunch.

No one rode immediately in front of the herd. In the course of a long drive the trail boss usually rode far ahead to survey the ground and search out watering-places and good grazing ground, but in this instance, a short drive over familiar terrain, it was not necessary. Riding near the head of the marching column of cattle were the point- or lead-men, working in pairs. When the course of the herd had to be changed they would ride abreast of the foremost cattle and quietly veer in the desired direction. The leading cows would swerve away from the horseman approaching and toward the one receding from them. Picked men occupied these posts for theirs was the responsibility of making sure the herd took the right course.

About a third of the way back behind the point-men came the swing riders. These were stationed where the herd would begin to bend when the course was changed. Another third of the way back were the flank riders. Their duty like that of the swing riders was to prevent wandering, and to drive off any foreign cattle that sought to join the herd.

Bringing up the rear, cursing the dust and the heat and the stragglers, were the drag riders who had to shove along the slow or obstinate critters and to look out for possible sickness or injuries. Drag was the meanest chore on the trail, but when, as in this instance, the cows were passing through a section cursed by widelooping, it was also a position of prime responsibility. It was the straggling rear of the herd that was most vulnerable to a sudden shrewd and determined attack that would cut out a number of animals and race them into some canyon or gorge where pursuit would be hazardous for those not familiar with the lay of the land.

Following the herd in a long drive would come the "remuda"—spare horses in charge of the wranglers. In this case no remuda was necessary.

Last of all came the chuck wagon or wagons. The cooks were the drivers and before noon both vehicles forged ahead, attended by a couple of hands, so that the chuck would be ready when the herd caught up with the wagons.

As the herd rolled southward, Hatfield studied Wilson Brant. He was more and more convinced that Brant was the man who headed the band of owlhoots the evening Bill Carter was shot. Little things hitherto unnoticed assumed significance: the way Brant sat his hull, the way he managed his horse, his peculiarly upright posture and his easy grace in the saddle.

"He's my meat, all right," the Ranger mused, "but the question is, how to get him on the table?"

Of Chuck Taylor he had not the least doubt. He was certain that in all Texas there couldn't be two riders who rode with that particular shoulder motion. There were certainly not many squat, hulking two-hundred-pounders who could manage Taylor's gait.

The western sky was flaming scarlet and gold and the pale hush of twilight was descending on the range-land when the herd rolled into town. Soon the loading pens were packed and along the railroad siding all was orderly confusion as the cows were tallied, weighed and shoved into the waiting cattle-cars. Tim James, highly pleased, wrote out checks for the various owners and thanked them for not letting him down. Then the cowhands headed for the saloons, dance halls and other places in search of well-known diversion.

Hatfield, John Gaylord and Wilson Brant entered the Rocking Chair saloon together.

"I figure to spend the night in town," said John. "My old bones ain't up to another ride tonight. What say, Hatfield?"

"Think I will too," the Lone Wolf agreed. "No hurry to get back to the spread now that everything's taken care of, and I expect I'd better keep an eye on my hellions or they'll never get back."

"Let's sign up for rooms right now," suggested Gaylord. "Big crowd here tonight and if we wait we'll likely be out of luck."

Hatfield nodded and they walked to the far end of the bar to sign the register.

"How about you, Brant?" Gaylord asked.

"I think I'll ride home tonight," Brant decided. "I have a shorter ride and a better trail than you fellows and I have work to do in the morning." He leaned against the bar as Hatfield and Gaylord signed for rooms.

"Yours is second from the head of the stairs, on the left," Bob Baker, the owner, told Hatfield. "John, you take the one two doors down on the same side."

"I'm going up to wash off some of the dust before I eat," Hatfield said.

"Good notion," nodded Gaylord. "I'll go up, too."

"Soap, water and towels in the rooms," said Baker. "Want some water heated?"

"Cold will be good enough for me," said Gaylord. "I'm hungry and don't want to wait. Okay with you, Jim?"

Hatfield nodded and they went upstairs together. With the assistance of the light streaming through the open door from the bracket lamp in the hall, Hatfield located his own lamp, lit it and shut the door. He glanced about, taking careful note of his surroundings as was his habit. He saw that just outside the window grew a big tree with a stout branch paralleling the window sill and almost touching it.

"Would come in handy in case of a fire," he chuckled as he poured water into the basin. "And some ossified gent is likely to set one any time in this old wooden shack. She'd go up like a patch of dry grass."

When Hatfield and Gaylord descended to the saloon, Brant and Chuck Taylor had already downed a snack and departed.

"There's an empty table in the corner," said Gaylord. "I'm hungry enough to eat one of my own cows raw."

They enjoyed a leisurely meal and then smoked and had a couple of drinks. Finally Gaylord stretched and yawned. "I'm going to bed," he announced. "I'm tired as hell."

"Think I'll stick around a while and keep an eye on the boys," Hatfield said. "I see most of them are in here."

Gaylord said good-night and stamped out. Hatfield ordered another drink and rolled another cigarette. An hour or so later, satisfied that everything was under control and that the Cross C bunch was no drunker than usual, he headed upstairs to bed. He reached his room and was about to turn the doorknob when abruptly he jerked his hand back as if the innocent bit of metal was the head of a venomous snake. The door that he remembered closing before going down was slightly ajar.

Standing perfectly motionless, Hatfield listened intently. There was no sound inside the room that he could catch, but the ominous crack seemed to glower threateningly. It was dark inside the room and the light was behind him. If he opened the door he would be a sitting quail for anybody holed up in there.

"And that tree branch right outside the window would provide a mighty convenient get-away," he muttered. "I don't like it. I know damn well I shut that door before I went downstairs."

Of course the door might have been accidentally opened by some guest seeking his own room and getting confused, but Hatfield preferred to take no chances. Too many ominous things had happened already. He considered the door a moment, then moving with the greatest care, he flattened himself against the wall, reached far out and seized the door knob. With a quick jerk he flung the door wide open.

The building rocked to a crashing explosion. A double charge of buckshot stormed through the opening and imbedded in the far wall. Hatfield paused by the doorway like a great cat about to spring, a gun in each hand.

Inside the room all was suddenly silent—no running feet, no scuffling, no sound at the window. All along the hall doors were opening, voices shouting excited questions. There was turmoil in the saloon below, then the sound of footsteps on the stairs. Hatfield holstered his guns and moved toward the open door, through which wreaths of blue smoke were drifting. Old John Gaylord came storming out, half-dressed, his old Russian Model Smith & Wesson at full cock.

"What the hell's going on?" he bellowed.

"Find out in a minute," Hatfield told him as cautious faces appeared at the stairhead. Confident that only a stark, staring lunatic would have stayed in the room under the circumstances, he took a chance and peered in. He stood staring at the devilish contraption strapped to a bedpost and glaring straight at him with twin black muzzles. Gaylord, looking over his shoulder, let out a roar of profanity.

"A sawed-off shotgun, trained on the door!" he bawled.

"Fastened to the bedpost," Hatfield said, "with a string running from the triggers down under the bed rail and to the door knob. Anybody opening the door and stepping in would have got a double load of blue whistlers. If the sidewinder hadn't left the door open a crack for light, and then forgot to close it before he slid out the window, I'd have opened it."

Gaylord swore again. Others joined in. Bob Baker came pushing through the crowd that packed the hall and took stock of the damage done.

"Wall will need a little paint," he decided. "Want another room, Hatfield?"

"Can't see as this one's been hurt much," the Lone Wolf replied, pinching out his cigarette. "I'll just cut down that scattergun and she'll be good as new."

He carefully examined the straps that held the weapon in place. "Part of an old bridle, I'd say," he announced, "and this is an old gun. Put it in the safe downstairs, will you, Bob? I'd like to have it for a souvenir."

"You came damn near getting a double-handful of souvenirs," Baker growled, looking askance at the shot-pitted wall. "I don't know what the hell this section is coming to. Don't see any notes laying around with 'Compliments of Jack Richardson' on 'em, do you?"

A sudden silence blanketed the crowd. Men glanced furtively over their shoulders at their neighbors.

"Good night, folks," said Hatfield. "I'm going to bed." He entered the room and closed the door.

Before lying down Hatfield carefully examined the window ledge and the tree branch that rubbed against it. On the branch he found a scuffed place where the bark had been scored by a boot heel. The side of the building fronted on a dark alley in which the tree grew and beyond the tree was a blank wall. A perfect set-up. Whoever set the trap had been thoroughly familiar with the ground.

"Which means he's around here frequently," Hatfield deduced. "Another twist in the twine. Wilson Brant was standing right beside me when I registered and knew which room I'd occupy. More nice circumstantial evidence that wouldn't stand up in court! But I've a notion he's getting jittery. This last slip-up will make him more so, and a jittery gent is easier to fool. Guess it's about time for me to make my throw."

He smoked another cigarette, shot the bolt on the door and went to bed and slept soundly.

21.

THE FOLLOWING MORNING Brad Dwyer rounded up his bleary-eyed hands and set out for the Cross C. Hatfield elected to remain in town.

"Got a little chore to attend to," he told the range boss. "I'll see you tonight."

Hatfield however did not remain in town many minutes after the Cross C hands had departed. He got the rig on Goldy and rode southeast. He didn't draw rein till he reached Tom Kane's ranchhouse.

The Diamond T owner greeted him with enthusiasm. "What's on your mind, feller?" he asked. "I been doing just as you told me to—sticking around home most of the time and watching my step. Nothing's happened."

"That's good," Hatfield replied. "If it had, the chances are you wouldn't have known about it, not in this world. Get your horse and let's take a little ride down to the southwest corner of your holding."

Kane bellowed for a wrangler and a little later they rode off together. Down where the hills walled the basin to the south, Hatfield pulled up and studied the ground.

"Rather dry down here," he commented.

"That's right," agreed Kane. "Nothing but salt springs down here."

"A little water would help," Hatfield said. "Tom, do you mind gambling a little?"

"Gambled all my life up until recently and it never got me anything but trouble," Kane grinned. "But I'll take a whirl at anything you say."

"Okay," Hatfield nodded. "You once said you'd string along with me and help clear up the mess in this section. Here's your chance. I want you to order a drilling rig from Del Rio, have it sent out pronto and start drilling down here. When we get back to the ranchhouse, I'll write out a list of what you'll need and I'll show you how to operate it. And I want you to spread the word around that you figure to tap an artesian well down here to take care of this dry range. Okay?"

"I said I'd string along with you and I will," the rancher returned dubiously, "but it'll cost a lot of dinero. I ain't got over-much and I don't want folks saying I married Mary for her money."

"Well," Hatfield smiled, "you can never be absolutely sure of such things, but unless I'm making a big mistake, and I don't think I am, you won't need to worry about that angle. You'll have plenty of your own."

"Now what the devil do you mean by that?" asked the bewildered Kane.

"I mean," Hatfield replied, "that while you're spreading the word around that you're drilling for water, you'll really be drilling for oil."

"*Oil?*"

"That's right," Hatfield said. "Unless I'm fooling myself, there's an oil pool, a big one, under this basin. All the signs point that way. The hills to the north are kerogen shale, from which oil can be extracted by heat and pressure. There are numerous salt springs. And those low hills that dot the basin are salt domes. All the geological features point to a subterranean accumulation of petroleum. I've seen this sort of thing before. The most favorable situation for the accumulation of oil and gas is where some structural irregularity, such as an anticline, or arch, in porous rocks, is capped by impervious beds. Gas will gather in the pores of the highest parts of the reservoir rock; below it, as on the flanks of an anticline, you'll find oil. Below that there'll be the salt water that's usually associated with petroleum and which often works to the surface to form salt springs. Porous sandstones and cavernous limestones—here you have both—not far from kerogen shales usually mean oil deposits, or oil pools. This basin was probably once a great lake or inland sea, millions of years ago, providing excellent conditions for the formation of oil. Clay or shale containing oil and gas will retain them in the fine pore spaces unless they are forced out by pressure, or by the superior capillary attraction of water. When they are forced out, the petroleum and gas will naturally circulate through the most porous formation available, such as sandstone, fissle shale, or cavernous limestone. Because both gas and oil are lighter than water, and water is found in most buried rock strata, they will migrate toward the surface and be lost. Shale beds, igneous dikes, salt domes and faults serve as excellent barriers. All those conditions prevail in this basin. Tom, I've got a mighty strong hunch that you're due to strike it rich."

"Sort of hard to follow, but I get the general idea," Kane admitted.

"That's why somebody is so damn anxious to get hold of your land—may have a fortune under it," Hat-- field added.

"You mean my brother?" Kane asked heavily.

"Your brother," Hatfield replied, "is, I think, the tool of a much smarter and more dangerous man. I don't know how much he's involved in the lawlessness that's been plaguing this section, but there's no doubt but that he's mixed up in the scheme to get your land."

"Jed and me never did get along together," Kane said, "but it's hard to believe he'd go in for robbings and killings."

"Flouting the law is just like any other bad habit," Hatfield replied. "It grows and grows. A man steps outside just a little, with an eye to easy money. But each time he gets just that much farther away from the straight trail. Soon he's in the same position as the jigger who caught a bear by the tail: he'd like to let go, but he can't. Perhaps he's got tangled with others and has to string along with them to save his own hide. I'm very much afraid that's the case with Jed."

"I'm afraid so," Kane admitted. "And you think that drilling the well will bring them into the open?"

"I do," Hatfield said. "I figure they'll go to any lengths to keep you from finding out what may be under your land. And they know that if you drill for water you'll very likely strike oil, if there's any here, for the oil would be above the water. Their natural objective, of course, will be to destroy your work and your machinery, figuring that you'd hardly invest in another rig. That's what I'm counting on, and I only hope the big he-wolf of the pack handles the chore himself. I think he will. Too important to delegate to a hired hand. We'll be waiting, and we'll grab him.

"The whole thing depends largely on your putting over your story, that you're drilling for water. I believe it'll work. It's not illogical. You've got a lot of fine range going to waste down here for lack of water. Won't look unreasonable for you to invest some money in something that would pay off in the end."

"Okay," Kane said. "I'll do it."

"Fine!" Hatfield answered. "Now we'll ride back, to the ranchhouse and I'll make out a list of what you need. Telegraph the order to Del Rio and you should have the stuff in a few days. As soon as it arrives send me word and I'll ride down and show you how to set it up and get it going."

Mary was still up when Hatfield arrived at the ranchhouse, some time after dark. "Come out to the kitchen and I'll make you some coffee," she said. "Wilson Brant was here today. He asked about you."

"I'm not surprised," Hatfield replied dryly. Mary looked puzzled, but he did not continue.

"He acted funny, I thought," Mary continued. "Once again offered to lend me his range boss if you should happen to take a notion to leave or if I wasn't satisfied with you."

"What did you tell him?" Hatfield asked.

"I told him I was more than satisfied."

"With my work I presume you meant."

"That's right, now!" she complained. "Get me all bothered again! Tomcat!"

" 'I could not love thee so, dear, loved I not honor more,' " Hatfield quoted smilingly.

Mary sniffed. "Huh! There isn't any honor, or conscience either, where a—a—oh, go to the devil!"

Hatfield shook with laughter and refrained from continuing a discussion that he knew could very easily lead to complications.

Hatfield was toying with a hunch. The next morning he decided to play it.

"I can't get that darn canyon out of my mind," he told Goldy as he cinched the saddle in place. "I mean the one those two hellions slid into the morning we trailed Gaylord's widelooped herd to the Rio Grande. I figure they must have had a reason for heading for that crack instead of across the River with the rest of the pack. I'm pretty sure that the one who got away was Chuck Taylor. We'll just amble down and give that hole-in-the-wall a once-over."

But Hatfield's real purpose was to discover if Wilson Brant and his bunch had a secret hide-out somewhere. It was highly unlikely that Brant would use his ranchhouse as a hangout for his outlaw band. Hatfield had studied his cowhands during the course of the round-up. They were, he decided, an average bunch of punchers with little thought beyond the ways of beef critters, barkeeps, and dance-floor girls. They were not the sort to ride out on desperate ventures outside the law. And Brant would hardly mingle his owlhoots with them. It would attract attention, cause comment. No, he must have some hole-up where his men could lie low between jobs. Doubtless he never allowed them to drink and carouse in Bowman; there were other towns within riding distance. Brant would think of those things and act accordingly. If Hatfield could find the hidden hangout he might be able to bag the lot of them without resorting to the precarious plan he had worked out with Tom Kane. At any rate it was worth the chance.

Riding warily, keeping a careful watch on the surrounding country, he headed south through Kane's hill range. Once he was well into the hills he turned Goldy's nose to the west. From a tall ridge grown thick with brush he studied the land over which he had passed. Nobody, he decided, was trailing him.

"So far, so good," he told the sorrel. "We'll turn

south at the edge of Brant's holding and follow the broken ground south. Not much chance of being spotted there."

It was a little past noon when he reached the Rio Grande. Less than half a mile to the east was the canyon mouth. Again assuring himself that nobody was following, he entered the gorge, his vigilance increasing as he bored deep between the rock walls.

For several miles the gorge maintained a uniform width, then it began to narrow, the walls to increase in height. The going was rough and Goldy snorted his disgust as he skated over rocks and patches of loose shale.

"Made to order for a bunch that doesn't hanker to be seen," Hatfield told him, "and mighty slow going for anybody who's not thoroughly familiar with the ground.

"If we happen to meet a few somebodies coming out of here, we're likely not to enjoy it much," he added grimly as the semblance of a trail twisted between huge boulders and clumps of thicket. He eyed the towering walls and shook his head. It was beginning to look like his hunch wasn't a straight one. The gorge, while rough and rugged, afforded very little concealment for a cabin or even a cave. Ahead the walls were lower, indicating that the east mouth of the canyon wasn't far off.

And then abruptly Hatfield saw something that interested him. A ledge sloped up the south wall of the gorge. From where he rode it looked not more than a foot or two wide, but having had experience with such things, Hatfield suspected that it slanted inward and was considerably broader than it appeared. Where it began he could not see. The canyon wall was flanked by tall chaparral, but some hundreds of yards ahead it turned around a shoulder of cliff and either petered out or disappeared.

Pulling the sorrel to a halt, he studied the ledge for

some moments. Then he turned his horse toward the
south wall and sent him into the chaparral. Goldy
didn't like it, and snorted explosively, but Hatfield
urged him on despite thorns and obstructing branches.
A few minutes of floundering and they saw the cliff
wall through a last straggle of growth.

The ledge began a hundred feet or so to the west.
And on the ground at its foot were the indubitable
signs of horses' hoofs.

"Feller, I'll bet we've hit it!" Hatfield said. "The
growth is a bit thinner over here but it still hides the
beginning of that darn shelf. And a chance rider going
through the canyon would very likely not even notice
it. Just as I figured, it's broader than it looks. Be a real
nice place to meet somebody coming down, but here
we go!" He sent the horse scrambling up the ascent.

As he progressed up the cliff, the ledge slanted inward more and more and broadened. Soon he was riding in a sort of lane of stone and was invisible to
anyone on the canyon floor below.

He reached the shoulder around which the ledge
turned and saw what could not be perceived from below because of the overlapping configuration of the
stone. There was a crack in the cliff face not more than
twenty feet wide beyond which lay a little brush-grown
mesa that ended in a steep, wooded slope tumbling
southward.

Warily alert, Hatfield rode into the crevice. A dozen
yards farther and he was at the edge of the mesa.
There, a little to one side, shouldering the cliff, was a
roughly built but tight-looking cabin. To all appearances it was deserted.

For long minutes, Hatfield sat his horse in the
shadow of the cleft, staring at the building. Sunlight
was pouring through the window and he could make
out vaguely the interior. There was no apparent sign
of occupancy and his ears could catch no sound.

"If there's anybody in there, they must be asleep,"

he told the horse. "You just stay here, feller, while I take a quick look. I've a notion we've found what we came for."

He dismounted and crossed the few steps to the shack, his hands hovering over the butts of his guns. He reached the door, listened a moment then shoved it open and stepped in, ready for instant action.

There was nobody in sight, but there were plenty of signs of recent habitants. Rough bunks were built along the walls, covered with dirty straw mattresses and tumbled blankets. There was a stove in the middle of the room with coals glowing through the grates. Rifles stood in corners, saddles and bridles hung from pegs driven into the logs. Shelves were stacked with staple provisions.

"This is it, all right," the Ranger muttered exultantly, "and from the looks of that stove, somebody has been around here darn recently." He moved about the room, examining its contents. The rifles were loaded and he saw boxes of ammunition on a shelf. He turned quickly as he heard Goldy snort. As he faced the door a man loomed against the sunlight. Hatfield saw the gleam of a gun. The room rocked to the report and the tall figure of the Lone Wolf crashed to the floor, face downward, hands outstretched.

22.

HATFIELD LAY PERFECTLY MOTIONLESS, holding his breath. He knew his life depended on whether his quick move had fooled the outlaw. For a crawling moment of suspense, the man stood in the doorway, peering with outstretched neck. Then with a grunt of satisfaction he stepped into the room and strode forward. He yelled with alarm and pulled trigger as hands gripped his ankles and jerked his feet from under him. The bullet thudded into the floor scant inches from Hatfield's face. He lunged for the gun and got the fellow's wrist. At the same instant a throttling grip fastened on his throat.

Over and over they rolled in furious struggle, Hatfield clinging to the other's wrist, trying to draw his gun while the terrible grip squeezed the breath from his lungs. They crashed against the stove. Over it went, spewing hot coals in every direction. Some of them landed on a straw bunk which blazed up instantly. Clouds of smoke swirled and billowed.

Hatfield got his gun out, but with a lightning move the other dashed it from his hand. It clattered across the floor and out the door. A fist crashed against his jaw and red flashes stormed before his eyes. He ground the fellow's wrist bones together, jerking his hand downward. The man gave a muffled bellow of pain and his fingers twitched spasmodically. The gun blazed so close to Hatfield's face that the burning powder seared his flesh. Then the outlaw gave a mighty lunge, a choking cry and stiffened, his heels beating a queer, spasmodic tattoo on the floor boards. He had shot himself through the throat with his own gun.

Hatfield staggered to his feet, gasping and reeling. Flame was wreathing all around him. The air was thick with smoke. Shielding his face from the fire, he lunged for the door, tripped over the sill and pitched headlong. The first thing he saw was his gun that slithered out the door a moment before. Mechanically, he picked it up, cocked it and held it in his hand as he scrambled farther from the burning building. Another moment and he was inside the cleft where Goldy waited for him.

"Feller, if you hadn't let loose that snort, he would

have got me," he said. "I sure ducked just in time. Look —there's a water bucket overturned outside the door. Hellion must have been to a spring somewhere. And I left you standing out here in plain view for him to spot! Well, they say the devil takes care of fools and drunks. Sure was on the job today."

He jumped a foot as a gun let go with a muffled boom. Other reports followed in swift succession.

"Hell!" he growled. "Just those rifles getting hot in there and cutting loose. But we'd better be trailing before all that racket brings somebody. And it looks like my little notion of maybe jumping the bunch in their hangout has gone the way of all dumb notions. They haven't any hangout any more. They'll have to hole up someplace else. Chances are, though, they'll figure that cayote they left behind to do the cooking got drunk and set the fire."

Riding down the ledge was a ticklish chore and Hatfield breathed a sigh of relief when he reached the floor of the canyon without meeting anybody on the narrow shelf. He nosed his way carefully out of the gorge and headed for home in a morose frame of mind. Things weren't going as he had planned.

"Well—maybe the twine won't tangle the next throw," he muttered.

Three days later Tom Kane sent word that the materials had arrived. Hatfield rode down to his holding. Under his instruction the Diamond T hands assembled the tall derrick, set up the boiler and engine, and got the cable, drill and walking-beam rigged. Hatfield glanced up at the shining drill suspended several feet above the earth.

"A modified churn drill," he remarked. "New and very efficient."

"She cost plenty," Kane lamented. "Feller, I'm just about busted."

"Hope you won't be for long," Hatfield responded cheerfully. "And anyhow you're all set. When I'm gone

Mary will need somebody to run her big spread for her and I reckon you're elected."

"A hired hand! And with my wife the Boss!" Kane growled despondently.

"What other kind of wife is there?" Hatfield wanted to know. "Okay, we might as well fire up the boiler and get started. You say you spread the word around, Tom?"

"Sure did," Kane replied. "And feller, you been spreading things around, too. I was plumb flabbergasted when old John Gaylord came up to me and shook hands. Said he was glad to hear I was getting along so well and that he thought getting water on the range down here was a good notion. This time last week he looked at me like I was pizen."

"Smart folks change their notions when they have reason to, and old John was right there with a big ladle when they were passing out brains," Hatfield smiled. "I've a notion a lot of folks are going to eat crow before everything is done."

The Diamond T hands got a fire going under the boiler and stoked it with billets of wood. Soon the steam gauge showed sufficient pressure. Hatfield cracked the throttle of the hoisting engine. The ponderous walking-beam rose in the air, the cable creaked over the pulley at the top of the tall derrick, the palls clicked and the heavy bit fell, cleaving the turf. The walking beam jiggled on its pivot, the drill bit deeper and deeper into the earth with a rotating motion.

"That thing sure doesn't waste any time getting into the ground," commented Kane. "Look at her go!"

"She'll slow up when she hits the stiffer clay, the shale and finally the cap rock," Hatfield said. "But she's a good piece of machinery. Cuts a lot faster than a straight-drive drill. Well, keep her going. I figure we'll need to get down at least three hundred feet, maybe a bit more before we hit rock salt. If we do, after going through kerogen shale and showing edge water, you can just about figure the well will come in when we bust the cap rock. And I'm telling you right now, when you hear her start to come, get the hell away as fast as you can. I'd say there's high gas pressure here and very likely the spout will knock the derrick to pieces and chunks of steel and wood will be flying in all directions.

"This is perfect for bringing in a gusher," he added. "With the slope of the ground toward the hills to the south you've got a natural storage reservoir all made to order. Won't waste a drop while you're waiting to get her capped. That is," he qualified with a grin, "that is if we're not wildcatting a dry hole. But I don't believe we are. And," he added grimly, "I've a notion some folks won't think we are, either. I've got to make preparations for that. There'll be a little night shift on the job after a few days."

Hatfield rode to the Cross C, but two days later he was back at the scene of the drilling. Kane drew him aside.

"There's a hellion up there on the hilltop keeping tabs on us," he said. "I got good eyes and caught a glimpse of him yesterday and again today. Think he's figuring on throwing lead at us?"

"Not likely," Hatfield said. "Chances are he's just up there checking the progress we're making."

"Shall I try to root him out?" Kane asked.

Hatfield shook his head. "No, leave him alone. Let him go back to headquarters and report. You're not supposed to have anything to conceal and if you made an issue of that jigger snooping around they might get suspicious. How are you coming with the bore?"

"Okay," said Kane, "only not so fast as we were; seem to be hitting some pretty hard stuff, and it's getting wet, too."

"That should be edge water forced up by pressure," Hatfield decided. "A good sign. I'll take a look."

He inspected the bore and the bit. "You're in the

rock salt," he said. "After you drive through that you may come to some more shale or you may not. At any rate I'd say you're not far from the cap rock. When you hit that, the going will really be slow. Takes a lot of jiggling to bust the cap. Sometimes it's thick. But that bit will eat its way through it without any trouble. Once you start banging the cap you must be ready for anything. There is no way to estimate the thickness of the rock. You just have to be prepared for a break-through at any time. As I said before, I think there's heavy gas pressure in this area and if there is things are likely to get lively. I don't think there's any danger of the well coming in for a few days yet, though. But I don't know what sort of an estimate those gents keeping watch will make. Got to get ready for eventualities. You can look for some visitors with me when I come down in a night or two. Now I could stand a small surrounding and then I'm heading back to the spread. Got any word to send Mary?"

After eating, they smoked and talked for a while. Kane was in a loquacious mood and during the course of the conversation, Hatfield learned a good deal about Tom Kane's past life, especially the stirring chapter that dealt with his sojourn in and around San Antonio. Finally he said good-bye to the ranch-owner and rode north.

Twilight was gathering when he paused in the gorge of the Pecos where Bill Carter had been shot. He rolled a cigarette and sat gazing down at the hurrying water.

A strange river is the Pecos, winding and shining in the sun, a purple mystery beneath the stars. The waters of the upper Pecos are crystal-clear. Where they hurl themselves into the Rio Bravo, more than a thousand miles from its source, they are bitter and murky, as if they had been brined and fouled by the dark and bloody land they cross. Thundering in its sunken gorges, swirling through its broad lower valley, the Pecos covers a land of legend and horror, a country where anything can happen. Nowhere in the South-west, perhaps, has lawlessness reigned as supremely as in the trans-Pecos country. Nowhere have the Texas Rangers written a more brilliant page in a long history of successful warfare against the pests of evil.

And now, Hatfield felt, one of the strangest chapters of all was unfolding. A "dead" man risen from the grave. Brother pitted against brother in a bitter struggle with a fortune the winner's stake and death the loser's forfeit.

For Hatfield was beginning to believe that Wilson Brant might indeed be the notorious Jack Richardson. The magnitude of his plot, its cold ruthlessness and in-tricate ramifications were in the Richardson tradition, all right. Well, it didn't particularly matter. If Brant was not Richardson he was a legitimate heir to his bloody mantle and a formidable opponent for even the Lone Wolf.

"No law west of the Pecos!"—that's what they said. But law was coming to the Pecos—Ranger Law! With a last glance at the sinister stream that never gave up its dead, Hatfield rode on.

23.

HATFIELD DID NOT TURN OFF at the Cross C. Instead he rode on to old John Gaylord's *casa* where he received a warm greeting. Gaylord looked a bit startled when Hatfield voiced an unusual request.

"Sure I'll ride down to Tom Kane's place with you and the others," he consented. "But maybe those young hellions down there will look sort of sideways at me. We didn't used to exactly get along, you know."

"I think you can risk it," Hatfield smiled. "Anyhow I'm taking Brad Dwyer and old Pete along, too, and they should serve as a sort of balance wheel."

"Okay," agreed Gaylord. "Anything you say is okay with me. Day after tomorrow night? I'll be down to the Cross C in time for supper."

The following afternoon again found Hatfield at the scene of the drilling. He was anxious to check on the progress made.

"We been hitting something mighty hard all day," Kane told him. "Going through it, but slow."

Hatfield listened to the muffled thump of the drill deep in the earth. He took a sample of the boring.

"You're on the cap rock or I'm greatly mistaken," he said. "Any day now she should come in, if there's anything down there beside salt water. I'm more and more of the opinion that there is, though. I've a notion this time next week you'll be turning away folks who want to invest money in the development of your holdings."

"Have to admit it sounds too much like a fairy story for me to really believe in," Kane chuckled. "But, feller, you sure make it sound real. Say you'll be down tomorrow night?"

"Yes," Hatfield replied. "I think it's about time for us to widen our loop for the throw. Did you spot that watcher up in the hills again?"

"Uh-huh, he was down closer today," Kane said. "I gave the boys orders not to pay any attention to him or even look much in that direction."

"That's good," Hatfield answered. "I don't believe they've caught onto the fact that you're drilling for something other than water. But if they're going to make a move they'll be doing it soon. Whoever was smart enough to figure the value of this land must also be smart enough to realize that you must be close to the cap by now. Well, so long, I'll see you tomorrow night."

Kane and his hands were more than a little surprised the following evening when Hatfield rode in accompanied by John Gaylord, old Pete of the Cross C and Brad Dwyer. But they dissembled their surprise and greeted them cordially.

"Chuck's all ready to dish up," Kane said. "We waited for you fellers. Come right in. I'll have the wrangler take care of your cayuses."

"Done et already, but that was a few hours back and I reckon I can stand another helpin'," said Gaylord. "And these hellions with me are always hungry. Ever see a cowhand who wasn't? The way they eat is what keeps a ranch-owner poor."

After they finished eating, Hatfield gathered the bunch around the table and quietly told them what he knew and what he expected to do. His listeners were astounded as the story unfolded.

"Wilson Brant!" sputtered old John. "I'd never have believed it; he's always seemed such a nice feller—but the way you tell it, there ain't much doubt about it. Well, if this don't take the hide off the barn door!

"But, Hatfield," he added, "ain't this a mite risky, taking the law in our own hands this way? Hadn't we ought to have the sheriff or a deputy with us?"

"Isn't necessary," Hatfield replied with a smile, "for in about two minutes you're going to be duly deputized to assist a peace officer in the performance of his duty." He laid the silver star on a silver circle before them. There was an instant of stunned silence, then,

"A Ranger!" exclaimed Gaylord. "You're a Texas Ranger! Well, I'd ought to have knowed it!"

"And I got you placed at last!" squalled old Pete, hopping with excitement. "I know now where I saw you before—over to Franklin, at the Post, when I was there last year. You're the Lone Wolf!"

Jaws dropping, the group stared at the man whose exploits were the talk of the whole Southwest.

"The Lone Wolf!" repeated Tom Kane.

"I've been called that," Hatfield admitted with a smile. "And now hold up your right hands and we'll get busy. No telling when those sidewinders will strike, if they do, and we'd better be prepared."

Ten minutes after taking the oath, the posse rode to the site of the drilling and holed up in the thicket Hatfield had chosen. A heap of oil-soaked waste and brush lay ready for a match. Hatfield voiced a last word of warning.

"I don't think they'll be taken without a fight," he said, "so act accordingly. Don't take any chances. At the first move, let them have it. We'll do this in a lawful manner and give them a chance to surrender. But they get only one chance."

"The better way would be to mow 'em down soon as they show," growled old Pete. "The only good ones of their kind are dead ones."

"You've got something there," Hatfield admitted, "but we are peace officers and must conduct ourselves as such. But I repeat, don't take any chances. Wilson Brant may or may not be Jack Richardson, but he's smart and he's bad. One opportunity will be all he'll need to put *us* on the spot instead of him."

There followed three tedious nights of watching and waiting. And each day the churning drill bit deeper and deeper into the cap rock.

"I think you're going to get your well, all right," Hatfield told Tom Kane morosely, "but I'm beginning to wonder if I haven't sort of tangled my twine this throw. Wonder if the hellion figured out what's going on and is laying off? He's got plenty of wrinkles on his horns and I wouldn't put it past him. Well, all we can do is hang on till the well comes in or something breaks."

"You're doing the driving," old John said, "but I'm sure getting tired of this laying out at night. Bad for my rheumatiz."

The fourth night descended clear and still with a sky of stars and a slice of moon in the west that cast a wan radiance over the lonely prairie. At the site of the drilling all was dark and deserted. The tall derrick loomed starkly against the star-strewn sky. Midnight came and went, the moon sank lower, the shadows deepened, and nothing happened.

And then there filtered through the ghostly silence a faint muffled clicking that grew in volume—the sound of horses' irons beating the grass-grown prairie. In the thicket the hidden watchers tensed.

"Get set!" Hatfield whispered. "It's them, all right. Here's the showdown. Clate, get your match ready for that pile of waste. Light it when I nudge you. The rest of you ride with me and fan out with guns ready."

The sound of hoofs grew louder. Bridle irons jingled and saddles popped as shadowy horsemen pulled up beside the derrick. Hatfield counted nine in all. They dismounted swiftly and clustered about the boring over which hung the point of the motionless drill. Hatfield nudged the cowboy with the match and took a long stride from the concealment of the brush, Tom Kane beside him, as a sparkle of flame winked amid the group beside the well. His face was set like granite. On his broad breast gleamed the star of the Rangers.

Abruptly there was a flash, a crackling, a blaze of intense light that made the scene as bright as day. The huge heap of oil-soaked waste was burning fiercely.

The group around the derrick whirled to face the thicket. Foremost were Jed Kane, Chuck Taylor and Wilson Brant without his glasses and with two heavy guns sagging at his hips. Jed Kane's face was ghastly white. Wilson Brant's eyes flamed with mad rage.

Jim Hatfield's voice rang out: "In the name of the State of Texas, I arrest Wilson Brant and the rest for robbery and murder. Anything you say—"

The words were drowned by an animal-like howl from Brant. "Damn you, Tom Kane, I'll take you with me, anyhow!" he yelled and went for his gun.

He was unbelievably fast, but Jed Kane was even faster. He struck Brant's arm up and the bullet intended for Tom Kane's heart whined harmlessly over his head. Brant whirled and fired point-blank even as Hatfield's bullet struck him. He and Jed Kane fell in a bloody heap.

The outlaws had gone for their guns and were shooting it out with the posse. A man who had been bending over the bore with a bundle of greasy cylinders in his hand stood erect, then fell forward as a bullet struck him. The bundle of dynamite sticks dropped from his nerveless hand.

Hatfield ran forward, shooting with both hands. Chuck Taylor dodged behind a derrick support and answered him shot for shot. A bullet plucked at Hatfield's shirtsleeve, a second burned a streak on the side of his neck. A third turned his hat on his head. Then Taylor reeled back, pawing at his bloodied shoulder.

He turned, ran a few paces and fell, writhing and groaning.

Deep in the bowels of the earth sounded a muffled boom as the dynamite exploded. Almost instantly the explosion was echoed by a deep-toned, ominous rumbling that swiftly became a rushing roar.

"Back!" Hatfield shouted. "Back from the derrick. The dynamite busted the cap rock and the well's coming in! Run!"

Herding three prisoners before him, all that were left on their feet, he followed the possemen who were already in motion. They were still dangerously near the well when from the bore shot a black column, driving upward with irresistible force. The drill shot into the air. The derrick seemed to leap from its foundations.

Chuck Taylor had staggered to his feet. His face convulsed with rage and hatred, he raised a gun and took deliberate aim at Hatfield's back. The tall derrick leaned toward him like the reaching hand of vengeance. Down it rushed with a screech of rending steel. The very tip struck Taylor and hurled him to the ground, his skull crushed, his neck broken.

High in the air, the column of oil feathered out and fell to the ground.

"Watch those hellions," Hatfield told the others. Shielding his face with his arm against the spattering oil, he ran forward and dragged Jed Kane's body in the clear. He straightened up and gazed down at Jed.

"Went out like a man, anyhow," he said. "Guess blood's thicker than water."

Tom Kane knelt beside his brother and spread a handkerchief over his dead face. He was crying unashamedly.

Gaylord and the others had secured the prisoners. Hatfield walked over to them.

"I can't promise you anything, but if you'd unbutton your lips a bit and answer questions, it might save you from stretching rope," he suggested.

Two of the outlaws were grimly silent, but the third showed a willingness to talk. Hatfield drew him aside.

"I had everything figured out about right," he told Gaylord a little later. "Brant drygulched Bill Carter and then killed him in Doc Beard's office. He'd already taken Jed Kane in tow, promising him half of the fortune in oil he figured was under Tom's land if Jed would string along with him and help get the holding away from Tom. Jed had enough knowledge of the principles of engineering to see the possibilities once Brant had pointed them out. He agreed to throw in with Brant and I guess before he knew it he was one of the pack. Run with the wolves and you soon grow hair."

"Why did Brant kill Carter?" Gaylord asked.

"He had two reasons," Hatfield explained. "First, Carter, a smart oldtimer with considerable experience with owlhoots, was getting too close on his trail for comfort. Second, he wanted the Cross C ranch and figured that with Carter out of the way he wouldn't have much trouble getting Mary under his influence. For the matter of that, I think he rather liked her for herself, in his cold way. I've a notion he'd finally tumbled to the fact that she'd fallen for Tom Kane, the way he tried to do for Kane at the last minute. He'd have got him, too, if it hadn't been for Jed. Jed came through like a winner at the finish."

"Think Brant was really Jack Richardson?" Gaylord asked.

Hatfield shrugged. "Could be," he admitted, "guess nobody will ever know for sure. But he was just as smart and just as bad as Richardson ever thought of being. There's one thing that lends some credence to the story. Brant knew a lot about Tom Kane's past. It was Brant, of course, who started the stories about Tom Kane being in San Antonio gambling and dealing cards there and cutting considerable of a swath. And he dropped the hint that Tom might be Jack Richardson. Tom was in San Antonio when Richardson was operating in that section. He was gambling and dealing cards and he did get into trouble there, a shooting scrape over a poker game, and had to cut and run for it. That was what sobered him up. He had managed to tie onto some money and he went to work for various spreads and saved his wages. When he'd gotten a pretty good stake together he came back here and got title to his land. Brant seemed to know all about it."

"Does sound a bit funny," nodded Gaylord.

"All pretty farfetched, but there it is," Hatfield said. "Of course Brant might just have been around that section of the country when Tom was there and perhaps knew him as a gambler and a dealer. Then when he came over here he recognized him and used his knowledge of his past to throw suspicion on him. The oldtimers were already a bit hostile toward Tom for getting title to what they considered open range and were ready to believe anything that was to his discredit. And Tom, stubborn as a blue-nosed mule and with a chip on his shoulder, never took the trouble to do any explaining, which of course played into Brant's hands. Getting two factions on the prod against each other is an old owlhoot trick. Provides a nice cover-up."

Tom Kane came over and joined them. "Well, guess everything is about settled," he said wearily.

"Looks that way," Hatfield agreed. "Telegraph to Del Rio for a crew to come and cap the well and build storage tanks. Guess you won't have to worry about folks saying you married Mary for her money."

Kane smiled wanly. "Guess not," he admitted. "Poor old Jed! I'd have gladly given him half of it if he'd only come and asked me."

Hatfield stayed for the wedding. He shook hands with Tom, kissed the bride and rode away, a pleased expression on his sternly handsome face, to where duty called and new adventure waited.

"There goes the grandest jigger who ever walked on two feet," said Tom Kane. He grinned at his wife. "But just the same I'm sort of glad to see him ambling off," he added. "He's a mite disturbing to have around."

"He's nice, but he's a tomcat," Mary replied. "I prefer a dependable bear that will always be around when I want him."

Leslie Scott was born in Lewisburg, West Virginia. During the Great War, he joined the French Foreign Legion and spent four years in the trenches. In the 1920s he worked as a mining engineer and bridge builder in the western American states and in China before settling in New York. A bar-room discussion in 1934 with Leo Margulies, who was managing editor for Standard Magazines, prompted Scott to try writing fiction. He went on to create two of the most notable series characters in Western pulp magazines. In 1936, Standard Magazines launched, and in *Texas Rangers*, Scott under the house name of **Jackson Cole** created Jim Hatfield, Texas Ranger, a character whose popularity was so great with readers that this magazine featuring his adventures lasted until 1958. When others eventually began contributing Jim Hatfield stories, Scott created another Texas Ranger hero, Walt Slade, better known as *El Halcon*, the Hawk, whose exploits were regularly featured in *Thrilling Western*. In the 1950s Scott moved quickly into writing book-length adventures about both Jim Hatfield and Walt Slade in long series of original paperback Westerns. At the same time, however, Scott was also doing some of his best work in hardcover Westerns published by Arcadia House; thoughtful, well-constructed stories, with engaging characters and authentic settings and situations. Among the best of these, surely, are *Silver City* (1953), *Longhorn Empire* (1954), *The Trail Builders* (1956), and *Blood on the Rio Grande* (1959). In these hardcover Westerns, many of which have never been reprinted, Scott proved himself highly capable of writing traditional Western stories with characters who have sufficient depth to change in the course of the narrative and with a degree of authenticity and historical accuracy absent from many of his series stories.